A RANGER, A WOLF, and a REALLY BAD TENT

BY
CASSANDRA JOELLE

This is a work of fiction. Names, characters, events, and organizations are either the product of the author's imagination or are used fictitiously. While real locations may be referenced, all characters and events depicted are fictional and are not affiliated with, endorsed by, or representative of the National Park Service or any other government agency.

Any resemblance to actual persons, living or dead, is purely coincidental. While this story may reference universal human experiences and emotions, it is not intended to reflect or portray any real individual or event. Any similarities are coincidental and should not be construed as factual. The author created this narrative to entertain and explore fictional themes, not to imply connections to real-world people or occurrences.

Copyright © 2026 Cassandra Joelle

All rights reserved. No part of this book may be reproduced in any form or by an electronic or mechanical means, including information storage and retrieval systems, without permission in writing from the publisher, except by a reviewer who may quote brief passages in a review.

cassandrajoelle.com

ISBN: 979-8-9910488-8-0

Scriptures taken from the Holy Bible, New International Version®, NIV®. Copyright © 1973, 1978, 1984, 2011 by Biblica, Inc.™ Used by permission of Zondervan. All rights reserved worldwide. www.zondervan.com The "NIV" and "New International Version" are trademarks registered in the United States Patent and Trademark Office by Biblica, Inc.®

In their hearts humans plan their course,
but the Lord establishes their steps.
Proverbs 16:9 NIV

CHAPTER 1
IF I DIDN'T POST IT, DID IT HAPPEN?
EMBER

My phone had been dark for three seconds before illuminating again with a notification bell.

"Two new likes and a comment," I read the alert out loud, hoping, *praying* that one of them was from Graham Jones, my internet crush. We'd been flirting back and forth for weeks, liking each other's photos, and I thought I'd catch his attention with this new one. Afterall, I had only spent an hour taking the perfectly angled photo of my freshly pedicured toes in these new golden sandals. My fingers couldn't open the app fast enough, and my eyes and heart were quickly let down to see it was just a couple of random followers.

"Hey, @EmberHollis, can you recommend a place for a pedicure?" I tossed the phone onto my chair as I stood in my influencer-worthy closet. It was actually the second bedroom of my apartment that I covered in cheap shelving, but online, no one would ever know the difference. My phone buzzed again, and before it was over, it was back in my hands. This time, it was a text message from my mom, asking if I was planning on coming over this weekend after they got home from church.

My parents owned my apartment, which was the biggest blessing in my life. At twenty-four years old, I was able to live on my own in this hard economy and manage to pay my small portion of rent to them and some meager utilities with freelance work doing graphic design for a travel company.

After several minutes of texting back and forth, I set the phone down again, returning to staging my closet for my very first clothing brand deal. I had been very excited to get it; a small activewear company asked if I would help them market their summer launch of hiking clothes. The amount of times I have hiked in my life could be counted on one hand, but of course I said yes. They weren't after my ability; they were after my reach—all fifteen thousand of my followers.

Up until now, I'd only been getting free products in exchange for reviews and posts. This was my first paid gig, and I wanted to do it so well that many were sure to follow. I wanted to be the ultimate example of what a brand deal was. To forge a new path in the world of *influencing*. But there was just one problem: No matter how I laid the green and brown hiking clothes in my white, sparkling aesthetic closet, they just didn't go. It was one giant *cringe*. I didn't look like the kind of girl who would wear these clothes—with my long blonde hair and eyelash extensions—because I wasn't. I also didn't like the way they looked on—too baggy, not flattering. I held up the clothes to my slender frame; perhaps I could cinch them in the back for a photo?

After a few more seconds of thinking, I set the clothes down and sat in my pink velvet closet chair; one of those pieces of furniture that's mostly for looks. I opened my social media to scroll for inspiration, looking up some hiking hashtags. About two clicks later, I came upon a freshly posted hiking photo of a woman I'd seen a few times online before. *Nicollete Willis, 149k followers.* Her picture was of her on a large rock, looking out over the Serengeti as the sun was rising. A gentle wind was blowing through her long, lustrous brown hair. Her shapely figure was wearing spandex pants and white tennis shoes. Elephants could be seen grazing in the background.

As I scrolled down to read the caption, which I could bet was something equally awe-inspiring, my heart sank to my stomach's floor. Among her thousands of likes the photo already had, despite being posted only five minutes ago, which was ten minutes after I posted mine, it was *liked* by Graham Jones. I quickly took a screenshot of the evidence—you never know when someone will delete a post or remove a like—and went back to my profile. *"Hi, I'm Ember"* is at the top of my profile. My cheery, smiling profile photo that was professionally taken at a poolside retreat last fall in Scottsdale looked dull in comparison to the colors of Nicollete's picture. I clicked on my sandal photo and scrolled through each and every like and comment—sure enough, nothing from Graham.

I went back to Nicollete's profile. By the looks of it, she'd only just arrived in Africa, at least, it was her first post since arriving. My finger hovered over the "Follow" button, but I hesitated. Did I really want her to know that I was insecurely keeping track of her movements? Sigh. I followed her anyway and then set a notification for any posts. If I wanted to get Graham, I needed to see the kind of woman he liked. I could be that woman, right?

If only I had a scenic backdrop for photos. Here I was competing with *elephants*. Working for the travel company, I had made ads for many destinations, and I knew that my meager bank balance would not allow for such a lavish trip to another continent, let alone an expensive place. Where was somewhere I could go that was equally *wild,* beautiful, and most importantly, somewhat close?

CHAPTER 2
RING LIGHTS OVER REAL LIFE
EMBER

"Who wears white shoes in the Serengeti? Isn't it all like dirt and elephant dung?" My best friend, Traci, whom I'd been joined at the hip with since the first grade, handed me back my phone after looking at the post with equal concern.

"Well, I thought that, too. But everything she's wearing is a brand deal. Look—she's repped by this workout clothing company." I pointed to the logo just above her waistline, out shadowed by the tight clothes on her backside.

"Still… It's a little *skimpy* for the setting. Even if I had a butt like that, I wouldn't want to plaster it all over the internet. Besides, didn't you just get a brand deal, too?" she asked as she took another bite of her Caesar salad with large chunks of blackened chicken at our favorite restaurant.

"Yeah, I guess." I put my phone down in defeat.

"You guess, what?" She gave me a look.

"Nicolette's brand is better," I said in defeat. "The clothes are cuter. My brand is all loosely fit. Makes me look like I'm wearing a garbage bag in comparison." I picked at my Black Cod Picotta while the waiter came over and topped off our water for the third time without saying a word. I looked up from my phone as her sparkling diamond ring caught every form of light while she ate—sunlight from the outside windows, the overhead light and the reflection from the glass on the artwork around us. A constant reminder that my best friend was marrying a wonderful guy she met at church, and there I was trying to get a man online to notice me.

"If he doesn't ask you out this time, I'm going to lodge a complaint against this restaurant. This is why I like to come here—to see if he will finally work up the nerve." Traci watched the waiter, Ben, walk away and shook her head.

"Who?" I asked, looking over my shoulder. "Ben?" I gave her a confused look. We'd known Ben since elementary school, and he'd always been extremely quiet in an uncomfortable way. Sure, he was cute, but totally off my radar.

"Everyone knows that Ben has been in love with you since we were kids," she said, sounding annoyed.

"Well..." I didn't dare admit that was news to me. "That doesn't mean I like *him*," I said, defiantly. I looked back at him once more and caught his gaze. *No,* I thought to myself. "He's just not my type."

"And your type is what, exactly?" she asked, setting her fork down. Now that she'd been engaged for a month, to the guy she'd been dating for three, I'd felt she'd been trying to marry me off as quickly as possible and had less and less patience for my... dilemmas.

"Graham Jones," I said with stars in my eyes, handing her my phone back with his profile pulled up. The dreamy, blue-eyed, muscular man whom I'd been connecting with online all spring. He lived near the Arches in Utah and had quite the adventurous life. He was outgoing, God-fearing, and totally gorgeous. What more could I want?

"He looks short," she giggled. "Like, shorter than you, I mean. Which is fine, I guess, if you like that sort of thing." Furrowing my dark eyebrows, I took the phone back and gave his photos another look.

"He's not short. I'm only 5'5". You think he's shorter than *me?*" She nodded again, taking a drink of her lemonade as the rock on her ring finger glistened.

"Notice how he doesn't pose with anyone else. But that picture right there," her unpainted nail pointed to the screen, "where he's standing next to someone's bike? The seat comes up to his chest, practically." She lifted the wool off my eyes, and I saw immediately what she was talking about, but I shrugged it off.

"That's okay. I like *him*. Physical things don't matter in the long game," I said so fast that I prayed I would believe it wholeheartedly.

"You're right, Ember. Forgive me for speaking about his height." She gave my hand a squeeze as I still held onto my phone. "Now, what do you say we put the phones away and go for a little walk? I've got the bill." She waved over Ben and promptly handed him her credit card. Or rather, her fiancé's credit card that she got in tandem with the ring.

"Sure. Thank Chase for another great lunch, for me," I said with a wink. "But what does my phone have to do with anything?" Traci went quiet for a minute.

"I don't want to make a big deal out of it. But, you know, you're just *always on it.*" She looked away.

"I am not *always* on it, Traci. Look, here it goes in my purse. Away," I said, as I dramatically dropped it in my bucket bag.

"Thank you," she said, folding up the napkin from her lap and blotting her perfectly pouty lips with it. Traci was a natural beauty—no makeup, no eyelash extensions. No acrylic nails like me. It only made sense that she caught the attention of Chase Riley, from one of the richest families in Denver. They fell in love at lightning speed and made it official last month when he chartered a helicopter ride over the city. He had them land on a rooftop helipad where they took an elevator down to a private fondue restaurant. He got down on one knee, and there weren't even any pictures taken. That probably would have skyrocketed her to internet fame if there had been, but she didn't even have social media, often saying she didn't feel the need to share her life online. We were polar opposites in that sense.

I slung my purse over my shoulder, feeling my phone vibrate. Pulling it back out, there were no notifications on the screen. Traci looked away as she stood up.

"Sorry, I thought..." Putting it back in my bag, I got up and pushed my chair in.

"Have a great day, ladies," Ben, who's voice was much deeper than I'd expected, spoke behind us in a startling manner.

"Thank you, Ben," Traci said, smiling and looking at me.

"Yeah, umm, thanks." I looked back at her expectantly. What? Did she want me to go over and give him a hug or something?

We walked out of the restaurant, the warming late spring air kissing my face. Summer was almost here, and the store display windows were revealing shorter shorts, higher crop tops, and even more revealing footwear.

"Five years from now, the dress code will all just be string bikinis, by the way things are going," Traci said, shaking her head.

"I don't know," I said, "those crop tops aren't that scandalous, really. If you wear them with high waisted pants, you're not really showing anything."

"I just have a conviction to dress very modestly, is all," she said quietly, immediately turning to me. "But I'm not judging you in any way, okay?" She squeezed both of my hands. I knew Traci better than anyone, even family. I knew she didn't judge me. She was like a sister to me, and we could say anything to one another, but I did feel confused. Was she saying I wasn't modest? I shook off the thought.

"I know. Thank you for that." I looked down at my outfit; I wasn't dressed *immodest;* at least, I didn't think so. It was warm enough to go sleeveless today, so I wore a strapless maroon tube top that showed my tanning bed glow. It had a little crop to it, but not much, and I was wearing skinny jeans. Sure, they were skintight and showed every curve, but I'd always been slender, so I really didn't have curves to show. Nothing about it felt risqué. An uncomfortable feeling washed over me as Traci talked about her convictions. I'd never really had any of those, at least not for the simple things she had. I had a conviction that I didn't want to be in jail. Did that count? Before I could really hash it out in my mind, we walked up to a hiking store, and the internal lightbulb in my mind went on.

"Traci!" I hollered out as she stood right next to me.

"What?"

"This is what I need to do." We both looked up at the window where a mannequin was standing in an action pose on some fake rocks, and a sign advertised a blowout sale on gear.

"Become a window display model?"

"No. I need to go on a hiking trip. And then, I'll camp," I said, turning to her with my eyes as wide as they would go. Suddenly, the stars aligned as I remembered an advertisement I created for a lodge in Yellowstone National Park. There were buffalo roaming around a colorful, steaming geyser. Buffalo were just as good as elephants, I decided.

"But do you? I mean, you've never done anything like that before, and the wilderness is more challenging than you'd expect, and—" I let the door of the store closing behind me end our conversation as I started sorting through the discounted hiking gear. The bell chimed behind me a moment later as Traci begrudgingly entered.

"Yes, I need to do this."

"Are you sure about this, Ember? Maybe you should go with someone. I mean, I can't, with the wedding planning and all. Plus, I'm not really the camping type. I get eaten alive by mosquitoes every time I have dinner on a patio."

"I know, and don't worry. I'm not asking you to go with me. Besides, I'm never alone," I smiled, and she nodded.

"God is with you," she nodded.

"Well, yes, that too," I said, caught off-guard. "I was going to say, I have my followers. I'll be using this as one giant opportunity to livestream *and* advertise the hiking clothes. Of course, if I get the attention of Graham Jones while I'm there, so be it." Traci widened her eyes and nodded.

"I hope you know what you're doing, Ember. Please, please be careful." I agreed while I pulled out a tent that was 70% off of $100.

"I know exactly what I'm doing," I said, with the biggest smile of my life.

CHAPTER 3
I NEED THIS TO GO VIRAL
EMBER

The plan was set in motion, I thought, as I drove, recalling my day. I didn't listen to Traci when she tried to talk me out of it. She didn't understand what I was trying to do here, and from where she sat, I didn't know if she ever would. For some reason, her technology-starved life didn't include social media, and we had a hard time relating on topics of that nature. At this point, I'd accepted that she didn't like the same things as me. I didn't know if I could say the same for her.

Traci said she worried about me and the reliance I had on my phone and apps, throwing a lot of words around. "Addiction," being her favorite these days. But that was *insane.* Just because I used my phone for everything did not mean I was *addicted.* Addicted people went to rehab. Would I need to go to rehab for my phone? The idea was laughable.

After I bought the tent, Traci started firing off questions like a machine gun. "Where are you going? What do you know about camping? The area? The preparedness you need to be in the wilderness?" It took all of the strength I had to not roll my eyes at her questions. I wasn't really going into the *wilderness.* I was going to a national park, where people have spent time and survived for over a century.

"Yellowstone. It's perfect! It looks like an otherworldly place, but it's within a reasonable driving distance from here, and I'll be safe going alone. I can get what I need for my collaboration with the hiking clothing company, and maybe I can get something else." I smirked, knowing this was certain to grab Graham's attention. Before I knew it, Nicolette's Africa adventure would be old news. The cashier handed me my tent in a thick paper bag.

"People die in Yellowstone, too, Ember." Her statement stung. Off the top of my head, I couldn't see any reasons that would make Yellowstone dangerous.

"Well, I won't," I said with a shrug, unsure about my statement.

"No one intends to. But nature has a way of making itself known."

"I'll be fine. I've got a cute tent. I'll take plenty of food. Look, here are some dehydrated meals." I pointed to a rack of overpriced dinners hanging from hooks, grabbing some haphazardly.

"What about water to rehydrate them? Layers? Flashlights, batteries, space blankets?" Now it was time to shut this thing down. I was feeling frustrated with her questions, though I felt guilty for feeling that way.

"Look, Traci... I know you care about me and love me. I love you, too. But it's going to be okay. I'll camp in a campground surrounded by people. It's warm here, and that's not too far away. I think I'll manage just fine." Traci looked away, checking her watch.

"Oh, shoot. I better go. I'm running the refreshments for the youth group tonight, and I need to be there in an hour to start setting up." She leaned in and gave me a hug. "Just promise me that you'll be safe. Do your research. Yellowstone is gorgeous to look at but has many hidden dangers." I nodded, knowing she wasn't going to drop this otherwise.

"I'll be fine. I promise," I said, releasing from the hug and grabbing a jumbo-sized bag of granola. "With chocolate chips!" I exclaimed, pointing to the bag. She nodded.

"Okay. See you later, Ember." And with that, she turned and left the store, her beautiful, naturally shiny hair bouncing with every step she took.

"So, Yellowstone, huh?" The male cashier asked as he scanned my selections.

"Yeah."

"Whereabouts? I've explored a lot there. Of course, I haven't seen it all. Don't know that I can in this lifetime. That place is huge."

"I don't know yet. I was thinking I'd just get there and see about a campground." Admitting I had very little plans in the works to a stranger was harder than telling Traci.

"Hmm. Okay. I highly recommend you going online and getting a camping reservation and putting a plan in place. I mean, it's required, but that's how they keep track of you. How will they know if you do go missing or something?"

"Missing? What is this, the Bermuda Triangle? It's Yellowstone National Park for crying out loud!" I couldn't believe how Traci had reacted, and now this cashier, whose name tag read *Keynan* was echoing those concerns. He shrugged at my question.

"Your friend is right; it can be a dangerous place. But in my opinion, as long as you stick to the main roads and don't go dipping your toes in a random body of water, no matter how pretty it looks, you'll be fine." Finally, someone with some sense. I never intended to be crawling into a bear's den or swimming in a geyser pool. "It is still pretty early in the season, though," he said with a sigh.

"What do you mean? The weather won't be good or something?"

"It could always be bad in Yellowstone," he said with a chuckle. "But no, that's not what I mean. The roads are closed in a lot of places. You might have to drive all the way up North. The East Entrance might be open, actually. Let me check." He slowly typed on his keyboard, hunting and pecking for every letter. I pulled out my phone while I waited, and before I knew it, I was lost in a scroll looking for hiking picture inspiration. "The East is open. As well as the North, but the East is closer to us."

"Thanks, uh, Keynan." I swiped my card, ignoring the enormous number on the register. "You really went the extra mile." I smirked, trying to not blush at the total on the register. The food cost more than the tent! He gave me another bag and handed me the receipt.

"Have fun," he smirked, as if he knew something I didn't.

When I got back in the car, I put the destination in my navigation app, and I was floored when it calculated my driving time: *ten hours!* That was a long time to be on the road. But, if I played my cards right, I could get in and get out. If I left now, or at least, in the next half hour, after stopping by my apartment to grab the hiking clothes, I could be there by tomorrow. I could camp for one night, get all of my photos that I needed, and hit the road the next morning. Just a quick weekend trip, and I would be right back to work on Monday. Technically, I didn't have to work on Monday, since I was freelance. But after spending all of this money for camping supplies, it was imperative that I work as soon as I return.

Stopping by my apartment, I took the hiking outfit and put it into a small backpack. I also changed into a fitted t-shirt that was a tad bit sheer over my neon sports bra. But the sports bra matched my leggings, so I called it good. Topping it off with hiking boots that I'd barely taken the tag off of, I looked very sporty as I left for my adventure in Yellowstone.

CHAPTER 4
WI-FI FIRST, FACTS LATER
EMBER

Now, as I drove off into the sunset, my gas gauge was waning. I'd never been this far from my house on my own. My phone was propped up in a phone holder that was attached to my dashboard, giving me turn by turn navigation, and the beeps and chimes of my notifications were playing in the background. I glanced at my phone for each one. *One new like. Two new comments. Six new followers.* My fingers itched as I wanted to click on each one and see what they were. I knew I couldn't do it safely while driving and would have to wait. But the chimes kept coming. Then, a few texts rolled in. One from Traci. One from my mom.

Finally, the freeway had an exit coming up. I was in the wrong lane and surrounded by semi-trucks. I put my blinker on and waited for what felt like an eternity before I had a chance to merge and by the time I did, I missed the exit. "Next Exit: 3

Miles," the sign said above it. Okay, I thought. Three miles while I'm moving over sixty miles per hour; that's just a few minutes. I can wait. But during those three minutes, my phone sounded like a Vegas slot machine, and I couldn't take it anymore, clicking on my screen.

The colorful app loaded. I had my eyes on the road but looked over at it like the forbidden fruit that it was. Viral videos popped up immediately, filling my car with the comforting sounds of trendy songs. Just having the app open, I felt better. *In the know. Liked. Connected.* A horn honking pulled me out of my fog, as a semi-truck pulled in front of me. Woah. I slowed my roll, gently tapping the breaks. I couldn't see around the truck as I slowed further. The truck had its turning signal on, and I put mine on, too, knowing the exit was near. And when I did finally slip off of the interstate, I breathed a sigh of relief as I turned into a gas station just a few seconds later. It was one of those setups where it looped me to a giant rest stop that was scattered with semi-trucks, and then I could get right back on the freeway.

But the second I pulled into the station and stopped at a pump, I grabbed my phone. Holding it felt good. I checked all of my likes. The comments had unfortunately been from spammers, offering to share my posts on their profile for a fee. No thanks. And the new followers had been private accounts, all women. Great for me, but it appeared I didn't miss much. Then, I remembered I needed to check a few other apps and my email.

After an undetermined amount of time, the shock of my life came in the form of a knock on my passenger side window.

"Miss, are you okay?" A burly man who looked like he could be my grandfather asked with concerned eyes. I looked around my surroundings for the first time. Many people were looking at me, including a woman with children. Since the chances of my abduction happening here felt slim, I cracked my passenger side window to talk to him.

"Yes, I'm fine," I said, shrugging, but feeling a little embarrassed to have all of these eyes on me.

"You've been sitting here for forty-five minutes, looking down. We had someone just come inside worried that you were passed out at the gas pump," he said.

"Oh, I'm sorry. No, I'm fully conscious. I was looking at my phone." I held up the bright device to the man, seeing the woman who was probably the one concerned, who nodded her head and walked away with her children. "I didn't mean to scare anyone," I said, sheepishly.

"Do you need any help?" He motioned to the gas pump. "We like to keep things moving here. You're in the fast lane." His old hand pointed up to the big sign, that I didn't happen to notice when I pulled in, that indicated this was the express lane for fueling. People getting gas in a jiffy and hitting the road again. Not people who had been in a phone withdrawal and needed to check a few apps before getting out. I didn't realize it had been nearly an hour.

"I'm okay. Getting gas now. Again, I apologize." I unclicked my seatbelt and grabbed my wallet and jumped out of the car, hooking it up to unleaded gas as quickly as I was able. My hands were shaking from the fright and confrontation of it all. The man was kind, but it didn't cushion my embarrassment. Thankfully, I'd never see any of these people again.

While I was fueling, I could see my phone flashing from where it sat in the driver's seat. I needed to get out of here immediately, so I fought the urge to check it. As soon the gas pump clicked, indicating my car was topped off, I jumped back inside and got the heck out of there.

Another hour of driving proved tiresome, and I knew I needed to find a place to sleep tonight. So, I voice prompted my phone to find me the nearest lodging. "Rerouting. Take the next exit and turn left," the voice said. "Thank you," I said back to my phone. Sure, I might spend a little too much time on my apps, a thought that made me feel very uncomfortable, but technology was good. I wouldn't have known there was lodging here otherwise.

A large sign came into view that advertised all the things on the next exit, including restaurants and hotel brands. *Okay*, I thought. *I may have known. But now I'm prepared to make my exit, and I'm in the right lane and everything. This is still better than what I knew in advance.*

When I reached the bustling little metropolis in the middle of my route, I couldn't quite put a finger on where exactly I was. I looked at my phone to see that I'd made it almost halfway to the general area of Yellowstone. Pretty much what I had hoped for the first day, especially since I got a really late start on this last-minute adventure. I wasn't completely exhausted but knew it wouldn't hurt for me to stop and regroup for the evening, and I certainly didn't want to be out driving in the dark. I slid into a pull-off and decided my next move.

Pulling up the hotel websites on my phone, I found the most affordable option that didn't give me the creeps. The kind of place that has nice carpet that doesn't look like it holds an abundance of secrets. Artwork on the walls. A nice television. And most importantly, a strong Wi-Fi signal.

The place that checked all of these boxes for me was called *The Cowboy Inn*. When I pulled into the parking lot, the brightly lit building had a mountainous backdrop. I grabbed my things out of the car, including my tent so I could see the inner workings of it. That was me preparing. I lugged it inside under my arm, with my duffel back and bucket purse slung over my shoulder. A man in a cowboy hat was working behind the counter. I was unsure if it was the theme of the hotel or if he really was a cowboy.

"Howdy," he said to me as I walked towards him. He was sort of cute, I decided. The wooden reception desk had a horse carved in the wood and leather fringe hanging over the counter.

"Hi," I said. "I'd like a room for the night." He nodded, and I felt his eyes flash me a look a few times. Nothing disrespectful per se, but with Traci's words earlier about my clothing choices being more revealing than they should be, I was starting to feel a little self-conscious about it. It was the second thought today that made me very uncomfortable. But the brightness of my neon undergarments couldn't be dimmed, and

I realized I didn't have a jacket to put on. *I didn't bring a jacket to Yellowstone? I hope I don't regret that later.*

"I can do a junior suite double queen for $114.56," he smiled, which was less than I found online, so I quickly agreed. I paid, and he gave me the keycard with the room number written on its paper sleeve.

"Thank you," I said, to which he tipped his hat.

Once I got to my room, which didn't feel much like a suite, but it did have all of the things I needed, I connected to the Wi-Fi. "First things first," I said to myself.

CHAPTER 5
THE QUIET IS TELLING ME SOMETHING
RIDGE

"We got another one for ya, buddy," Travis Winters came up and set a fax on my desk. I analyzed the data from the Game & Fish department for the wolf we'd been tracking and nodded.

"Thanks. She's really on the move, isn't she. I'm just about set up now that I can track her digitally. You know, the radio collar is set up to track instantly." I gave him a knowing look. "I think we alone are keeping fax machines a *thing*."

"Nah. Have you ever had to send medical papers somewhere? Or, something for an insurance claim? Only faxes are allowed. Seems the more personal the information, the less security it requires. Why send a secure email, when you can send it to a printer in a big room full of random people? Big Fax has an *in* with someone to keep the machines going," Travis laughed. "It's good we have someone here who's savvy for a change. Those radio collars only started getting used in the last few decades and all of us old timers are still using dial-up internet." Then, he walked off. Though Travis acted like he was a curmudgeon in his late seventies, he couldn't be more than fifty.

Reaching for my coffee, I looked back at my computer with a squint. I wasn't used to all of this screen time, and it was killing my eyes. I rubbed them with my worn hands, calloused from my life working on the family cattle ranch just north of here. I'd always be a cowboy, but for now, the Lord was calling me here. To work in the most beautiful spot in God's creation and to care for His animals.

I wasn't here two days before hearing about wolf number 609, also known as Raya. Raya was darted, captured, and relocated to New Mexico for a large wolf reintroduction program that they attempted recently, along with the rest of her pack. Playing God never worked out, if you asked me, but here we were. All of the wolves were collared and traceable with radio transmitters. Most of them didn't do anything unexpected; they roamed around their new areas, found habitats, and made dens. Wolves are very social creatures, but Raya seemed to be defying all of that.

She left her unit almost immediately after transfer. Once the cages were open, and the wolves were freed from their transport cells, they were monitored for a few hours, and everyone packed up and went home. From there, no one in the region thought about it again until her beacon went off three days later, and she had made an incredible distance in the short time, walking over 120 miles away from her unit. Since then, Raya traversed over 1,000 miles her first month, back in the direction that she was captured from.

On my second day on the job, which was just a week ago, my boss Bob assigned me a new focus.

"Word on the street is you're a good tracker," Bob said, his voice raspy on the other side of the telephone hoisted to the wall, another modern marvel that we relied on out here in the woods.

"That I am, sir. I grew up hunting, trapping, and tracking prey that might be after our cattle."

"That's good. Well, I got a job for you, kid. Know anything about wolves?"

"Only what I've learned firsthand. We had a few worries with them after they were reintroduced to this park all those years ago." Flashbacks came in my mind of us trying to protect our animals from the wild creatures. I'd spent several nights on the porch with just the light of the moon to watch for a predator. Thankfully, we never lost any cattle due to a wolf. I didn't have a problem with wolves; in fact, I'd always found them to be beautiful, fascinating creatures that God created to complete His perfect ecosystem. But they are known to be ruthless when it comes to hunting.

"That'll do, son. Seems we've got one inbound. She's looking for something, and the scientists want to know what. Sure, they all wander, but these data sheets only go so far. The biologists are monitoring her remotely, but we need boots on the ground with experience to know what to look for when she returns. We know where she's going to go—no doubt, she's returning. But we want to know why. Who, or what, did we leave behind?" Bob was likely in his late seventies, but his passion for his job kept him going. So far, he was awesome to work for. Despite 96% of Yellowstone being in Wyoming, the offices were in Montana, so I also never had to see him or anyone else for that matter. The job was just what I needed for a break from the family business and plenty of quiet time to spend with God. "Call this more of my curiosity than the necessity of knowing, but I've never seen a wolf travel at this magnitude before."

"I'm up for keeping an eye on things, sir," I said. "Thank you for thinking of me." I hung up while I prepared for this new side quest. Wolves were known to roam. That's just what they do. But there was something intriguing about wolf 609; *Raya*. Hearing about her magnificent journey back did spark the wonders of my mind, and like Bob, I was intrigued.

Stepping outside of the small log cabin station, I looked out over Yellowstone Lake. Hard to believe that under the waters held a Super Volcano. There were so many interesting geological wonders in Yellowstone, that just being here a week, I didn't think I'd ever tire of it. This is the work I'd always wanted to do. The only downside was the hat on my uniform, as I much preferred a Stetson.

The winds changed as I stood in silence; I closed my eyes and breathed in the air, smelling the faintest hint of something burning. Opening my eyes, I scanned the shore. The lake was so large, it looked like the ocean, and the sandy beach that surrounded it felt like the real deal, too. It was the closest thing to the ocean that I would be getting anytime soon.

Spotting a family off in the distance making a small bonfire, I shook my head. We had designated fire pits for that. Still, despite my job title as a ranger, I knew I couldn't stop every knucklehead from doing all of the knucklehead things they were going to do. That would drain the life out of me faster than a big city shopping mall. No, I had to set boundaries for myself. The park was just now opening for the season, and there was going to be several months of tourists behaving badly, and I needed to pick and choose my battles.

"Woah, you going to do something about that?" Travis came rolling up behind me as he pointed to the family having an illegal bonfire on the beach. I just stared back at him. "Okay, I will," he shrugged, adjusted his hat, and zipped up his coat. There was a cool breeze today. I thought it was around fifty out, which felt great for me. At home, this would have been short sleeve weather. To Travis, whom I thought was from Florida if I remembered correctly, he was freezing his tail off. *Thank You, God, for making me tough.*

As Travis made the family put out the bonfire, I walked to the other side of the cabin. There were experiences kids should have growing up. Heck, I couldn't imagine not knowing how to start a fire or never having sat around one with my family. *Sigh.* That spot was just not the place. Travis eventually walked the family over to one of the designated fire pit areas, as I could hear someone's feet crunching through the site nearby.

*****

    My senses were high; I could hear, smell, and see things farther than most. I attributed it to never watching much television or having a cell phone. Instead, I'd spent my time tuned into the outside world and listening for God's voice. Right now, God was telling me to be still and listen. After several long minutes of scattered noises, most of which were coming from the tourists Travis was with, I heard what sounded like an artificial camera lens snapping. I walked all around the porch of the log cabin but didn't see anything. Finally, I stepped off the platform and walked twenty yards into the woods, holding my bear spray that was holstered to my hip, where at home, would be replaced by a pistol. When I was out in the backcountry of Montana, exploring the wilds, I had both bear spray and lead on my side.

CHAPTER 6
WORST TENT PLACEMENT IN HISTORY
RIDGE

In a small clearing up ahead, I finally saw what I heard from the porch. A blonde-haired woman who looked like she had mistaken Yellowstone National Park for a photography studio was standing next to a purple tent, talking into her phone. I resisted the urge to inquire, feeling an underlying general concern for this woman's well-being. This was late spring, in grizzly territory, when they'd just come out of their winter dens, and she was the lone tourist in the camping area.

Suddenly, all of those feelings about setting boundaries were out the window as I found my feet walking towards her. She didn't hear me walk up, which concerned me even more as I thought I was making as much noise, if not more, as a wild animal would.

"Excuse me, ma'am?" I said in a stern voice, to which she screamed and dropped her phone on a log. Without looking back at me, she scrambled to pick it up. All I saw was her blonde ponytail cascading down her back. She was wearing nice hiking clothes that looked moisture wicking and comfortable, but otherwise, her gear didn't seem very sturdy.

"Didn't anyone ever tell you that women don't like to be called *ma'am?*" she barked before turning to me. When she did, we both stood in silence for a moment, as she looked at me with the dirtiest look I'd been given in a long while, and I took her appearance in. She was undeniably gorgeous; and done up, yes. She looked like a woman that was *high maintenance.* Not the type of woman who could live off the land in a log cabin like I could. But her femininity was striking. Her bright, green eyes glowed against her tan skin. Her small frame looked like she couldn't fight off a fawn if it came after her, and I saw no sign of bear spray anywhere.

"My apologies, miss," I said, tipping my hat like I would in my Stetson. "I just wanted to ensure you were adequately prepared for camping here. You see that line over there in the brush?" I pointed to where the grass had been laid flat outside of the camping area. "This is a game trail. All of the animals walk this. Now, I don't know why the heck someone would let campers be here next to a game trail, but you're perfectly legal to sleep here. I just want to make sure that you've taken all of the necessary precautions so that you're safe doing so." And with that, her eyes softened a little from the defensive look she had been giving me before. That moment was fleeting, however, and she was back to whatever she was mad about.

"I'll be fine. I don't have any jars of honey." She crossed her arms, and I scoffed.

"There's no ego in the wilderness, ma—" I quickly corrected myself. My grandmother raised me to address everyone as ma'am, and I was finding it a hard mistake to correct. "Look, if you have any food at all, it needs to be strung up in a tree or in a bear proof container. Can't even be left in a car, I'm afraid. They will rip a door right off, if given the opportunity." A moment of fear flashed in her eyes before passing.

"I just have some granola. Will that attract anything?" She gave me a dull look, while her overexaggerated eyelashes batted at me.

"It can, absolutely." She shrugged.

"Well, I'll just throw them away, I guess." My heart was wrenched.

"I don't want you to do that. Here, let me show you how to hang up your food." And I did. I spent several minutes helping her with some basics, and when we were done, I looked at her tent. "Want me to reinforce anything on that?" I touched one of the poles, and the whole tent moved.

"No, it's fine. I watched a video tutorial before I came. It's set up correctly, thank you." Taking one look at this woman, anyone would expect a damsel in distress, not a damsel in defense.

"Okay, well, good. I'll leave you be. If you need anything, I'm just through these woods at the ranger station, about a hundred and fifty yards away." As I spoke, I surprised myself with how willing I was to be available to this woman.

"I won't, but thank you," she said. "By the way, where can I get a signal? No one told me there was like *zero* service in Yellowstone."

"I don't have a cell phone, but you might want to try Cody, the nearest town about fifty miles that way." I pointed to the West. "It's pretty sparse from here to there." As I spoke, she looked at me with disgust.

"I'll try the lodges. They probably have Wi-Fi."

"They certainly could, but most don't open for another two weeks," I said, pausing. "Here, at least take this." I unclipped the bear spray from my belt. She stared at it strangely before silently taking it out of my hands.

"Thank you," she whispered, not reaching my eyes as she held it in one hand, her phone in the other.

I wasn't even halfway back to the station when I heard her start back up again on her video.

"Okay, guys. So, I don't have any service here, but I'm about to go exploring and the second I find a signal, these will be shared. Can anyone guess where I am?"

*****

When I returned to the station, Travis was inside putting on another layer under his already heavy jacket.

"When does it start to warm up out here again?" he asked, smiling, but it did not reach his eyes. "You'd think I'd start to remember after all of these years, but the winters in Florida do not help me one bit, as my blood just gets thinner and thinner every year."

"We usually get some nice weather around the Fourth of July," I said, to which he let out a groan in protest. "Except for that year that it snowed, that is." I remembered it fondly—the

Fourth of July parade still went on. It was just a skiff of snow, after all, and the kids didn't mind. My folks didn't, either, as it meant they didn't have to irrigate that day.

"Why do we do this, again? Can you remind me? Nothing but annoying tourists." He had a touch of anger to his voice now, and I didn't want to fire him up by saying anything for or on the contrary. "Now I gotta go talk to the USGS about some volcanic activity, as I'm leading a talk on it later for these same annoying tourists." He rolled his eyes, and I turned away. His negative attitude was clearly a hurdle I was going to have to avoid this summer.

Turned out, the window in the ranger station cabin was a straight shot to the campground where *my* annoying tourist was staying. As I peered out into the wilderness, my eyes scanned for any movement that would let me know she was okay, knowing full well even if she wasn't, her prickly personality wouldn't accept help from me.

CHAPTER 7
NO SIGNAL, NO PLAN
EMBER

The drive up from Denver yesterday was gorgeous, once I made it past all of the freeways, anyway. I didn't know why more people didn't come here; sure, it was cold out, but living in Denver, with our icy cold temps all winter, this actually felt pretty good on my skin. If anything, it made me look even more tanned with the dullness of the colors behind me; the sun had not greened up the park yet. At least, from the brochures I got in the hotel I stayed at last night, it gets pretty vivid green here in the warmer months.

According to the information I read online, I could camp in a designated campground without a permit. When I got to the gate of Yellowstone and paid my entrance fee, the woman gave me a concerned look.

"Just you?" she asked, scanning my Subaru Forrester as if I was hoarding a family of five under the seats.

"Yep. Why? Is it cheaper if it's just me?" I asked.

"Nope. One flat rate per vehicle. Just wondering, that's all." *She must be writing a book*, I thought to myself, as she scanned my driver's license and gave me a park pass.

"Thanks," I said, begrudgingly. Rolling up my window, I slowly drove through the park, looking for signs for open campgrounds.

The first dozen I drove by were closed. This gate in the park had been open for a week. Why were the accommodations not? I pulled off into the parking area and pulled out my phone. Just holding it in my hand felt good after a long drive; I didn't care what Traci said about my phone use; this thing was so much more than that. It was a map. It was a phone book. It was an encyclopedia of the universe. It even had a Bible downloaded on it for offline use, not that I was ever offline. But if I was stranded on a desert island, I could read the Bible, until my phone went dead, that is. You'd think Traci would be impressed by that.

I opened up a web browser and typed in, "why are campgrounds closed in Yellowstone in May," hit enter, and for the first time in the history of having a cell phone, nothing loaded. I hit refresh three times before I noticed something truly horrific: I had no cell service.

The thoughts immediately creeped into my mind; what if I had an emergency? What if I needed help? I didn't even tell my parents I was doing this. I left in such a haste, bringing with me those stupid outerwear clothes and my new tent that I didn't even have time to do any research on the cell phone towers in the area. But why would I have even thought for a minute there wouldn't be any cell phone reception? This was America, after all! The great states of the U.S.A.! Who would have ever thought there would be unchartered territory where my cell phone wouldn't work? For crying out loud, Nicollette's cell phone worked in Tanzania!

Pulling back out into the road, I considered that maybe this was just a dead zone. I had been in those before, like when I was driving through a long tunnel, or when I was in a basement or at that hair salon I used to go to that had the metal roof that made cell phones useless bricks. I switched to another place after that experience; no sense in having a relaxing hair day refresh if I couldn't even check my socials for four hours.

As I traversed the winding park roads, many signs alerted me of scenic viewpoints, pull-offs, and geological wonders, but I couldn't think straight as I wondered when the last time my phone had pinged my location? If my mom checked where I was today, she'd think I'd been taken. I should have called her when I was at the hotel last night, sure. But I was too consumed with learning how to set up the tent from that online tutorial! I must have watched it five times, plus I practiced in the room. It was a small tent, for easy carrying and even easier assembly. And then I was busy checking in with my followers. Scanning my posts. Re-reading my captions. Curating my online image was a full-time job.

Now, I was filled with regret that I didn't check in anywhere beforehand. Then, I saw it, like a mirage in the desert: a gas station with a small general store. Surely, they had cell reception or Wi-Fi, right?

I couldn't pull in fast enough. Parking sideways, I took up multiple spots, but no one else was around. Who would have cared? I didn't even take my keys out of the ignition when I broke into a run to get in the store, but when I reached for the handle, my heart sank again, as I read the sign on the door: *Closed until May 15th.* As I wallowed in my panic, I considered turning around and driving back into civilization. I was only four or five hours away from the hotel I had stayed in last night; and I did drive through a little town this morning. Surely, they had cell phone service. That was only two hours from here, give or take. Would that really be so bad? No, I didn't think so. Better than the alternative of just falling off the face of the earth.

As I trekked back to my car, I saw a relic of the past: a shiny silver payphone, untouched by the modern world. I went over to it, expecting it to not even work. But holding it up to my ear, I heard the most glorious monotonous noise: a dial tone. Racing back to my car, I dug around my purse for some coins and came up with seventy-five cents.

I held the coins in my palm, excited to dial my mom and let her know about the adventure I was on. I'd call Traci next and have her check my socials to see if my latest post had any likes. She wouldn't like doing that, as she would have to look it up on her computer since she didn't have any of the apps, but I knew she would do it for me. Then, with my last quarter, I'd call some park officials, and I'd figure out why the cell phone towers weren't working.

CHAPTER 8
NATURE IS NOT A BRAND DEAL
EMBER

When I returned to the pay phone, I was horrified to see that a call was no longer ten cents as it had been the last time I had seen one of these dinosaurs, but it was now fifty cents! I looked at my pathetic coins. I only had enough for one phone call. Momentarily, a flicker of wonder crossed my mind: what if I called Traci, had her check my socials, and then *she* could call my mom and let her know where I was? Ugh, I couldn't do that. I couldn't believe I would even *think* that. What was wrong with me? Was there any truth to what Traci said, that I was *always* on my phone?

My mom answered on the second ring. "Hi, mom," I said. "I don't have much time because I'm using a pay phone."

"A pay phone? Wait, is this your 'one call' from prison?" There was a slight tone of humor in her voice.

"I'm in Yellowstone. Spur of the moment trip, and apparently, they don't have very reliable cell reception here." I put my head in my hands as we conversed about the park. She went on and on about the beauty, having been there once before I was born.

"I'm so happy for you, Ember. I hope you have a wonderful time, but please, be safe. Stick to the tourist areas. And check in with me tomorrow. Don't make me worry about you, okay?" Her voice was sweet as syrup, and I agreed to call her again when I found the chance to do so.

"I'm sure there's an ATM around here somewhere. If I have to, I'll drive out of the park to find one." My heart picked up the beats as I considered how good it would feel to regain the use of my phone, just as the payphone alerted me my money was running out. I held my last quarter in my hand, wondering if I should save it for later.

"Well, I'll let you go, sweetie. I can't wait to see the pictures. I guess this means no church on Sunday?" she asked, and my gut filled with guilt once again. I couldn't even remember the last time I attended with her, letting her down. There was always something going on with me, or sometimes, I just needed the mental health day.

"I'm sorry, I—" and the call was cut off. "I forgot," I finished my sentence. Hanging up the phone back on its hook, I walked away. Truth was, I'd forgotten church a lot lately. It wasn't that I didn't believe in Jesus; I did. It's just that I'd been... distracted. I looked down at the useless phone in my hand. "Distracted by this," I said, as I unlocked it once more to see if it magically had a bar of service, but still, nothing. At least my mom knew I was safe. Traci could always get in touch with my mom to see where I was. I was less worried about contacting her than I was checking in with my followers and realizing that made me feel weird.

My followers and online platform gave me something that I hadn't found anywhere else: the feeling of being chosen. Seen. Preferred. And that validation was just too good to give up.

It was almost two in the afternoon when I finally found a campground that was open. It wasn't as scenic as I hoped—in my head, I had pictured a tent by a river. Maybe buffalo would be roaming around as I drank my steaming coffee that I brewed over the fire. Dang it, I should have watched a video on how to start a fire. Anyway, that didn't matter. I had a lifetime supply of granola and on the drive here, I saw that they serve coffee at rest stops. So, I was certain that there was *somewhere* that would pour me a cup of coffee in this large swath of a tourist destination. Right?

Pulling the gear out of the back of my Forrester, I picked the perfect spot. It was surrounded by logs that were great for posing on. The aesthetic was real; sure, from in the woods you couldn't even tell that I had driven nine hours to be here. At first glance, it looked like I was in the wooded area behind the dog park. I didn't think to snap a picture of the sign when I entered the park this morning, and now I was kicking myself. So, I pulled out the brochures from the hotel I stayed in last night and set them on the log and took some artful pictures. There. That would do it.

After I was done, I assembled the tent that now, out in the wild, didn't seem as secure as I thought. Still, I was pleased nonetheless, and now it was time to get some videos whether I had service or not. I'd just have to post them later. I slipped into my tent and changed into those drab hiking clothes from my brand *collab*. I needed to make it look natural that I was wearing them. I fluffed my hair and put it into a high ponytail. I was fresh faced, and thanks to my eyelash extensions, I just needed a little bit of rosy bronzer on my cheeks to give me a made up look that was still natural.

Outside of my tent, I started filming.

"Hey guys, it's Ember," I said, moving around to find just the right lighting. It was a little overcast here in the woods, but outside the tree line, the sun was shining brightly. "I'm out here on a wild adventure, and I couldn't do it without Outdoor Trekking Gear clothes. Look at this new outfit from their spring/summer collection. It's loose so I can really move around." I started to trail off on the features of the clothing, really emphasizing how comfortable they were since they were not restricting my breathing nor were they skintight, all of the things that Traci implied I wore, and that weird feeling returned.

"Excuse me, ma'am?" A deep, *handsome* voice scared me into next week. I dropped my phone on the log, hearing a part of the screen break. I scrambled to pick it up and assess the damage. Thankfully, the small crack was just in the top corner that would not affect my vision on what mattered such as seeing if Graham liked my posts or not. Annoyed, I turned around and was flabbergasted at the obscenely gorgeous man standing behind me. He was so good looking that it made me angry, in fact. Angry, because here I was chasing a man that Traci thought would come up to my shoulder, and this man was almost towering over my small frame. *Why can't this guy be on my social channels?* Not that Graham was chasing me, per se. If this man wasn't a park ranger, I'd be concerned by his striking aura that exuded a certain prowess that I'd never in my years experienced until now. There was something about this guy that was so masculine... I didn't even know what to do with myself.

I didn't have to think long about what to do, however, because he started asking me questions. It wasn't that he was talking down to me, but I thought this *cowboy* type thought that I was a damsel in distress. As if a girl like *me* couldn't shake it in the woods by herself. He started asking me questions. Was my food out of reach from the grizzly bears? Was my tent secure, or did I need him to double check it for me? Just looking at him was incredible. His hands looked like he could pull in an anchor from the bottom of the ocean floor. His arms, despite wearing a long sleeve shirt, bulged like he just bench pressed a cow moments before. His eyes, the clearest green gems I'd ever had gazed upon me, saw right through me, and I hated every second of it.

I dismissed him at every turn, surprising myself in the process. At home, if a man this striking, or even a fraction of this approached me, I'd be all ears. Not that it was about looks—I wanted the full package. But there was something about this guy that made me feel... irked.

Then he told me he didn't have a cell phone. What kind of world was this guy living in? I knew there was something different about him the moment I laid eyes on him and sure enough, he was one of those weirdos who wanted to be disconnected with the world. I just couldn't take that kind of life. Could I? What sort of meaning would there be if there was no internet? No followers? No "liking" photos to my heart's content?

After all that, he handed me a bottle of bear spray, which I accepted. Looking at the can gave me a reality to the situation that I didn't really have before. Not that I was foolish—I knew there were bears here. In fact, I was hoping I'd get one in a photo. Competing with Nicollette's elephants after all, remember? But the elephants weren't hunting her. They didn't seek out people to trample. *Did they?* I thanked the handsome ranger for the can, and he left.

I couldn't get the unsettling feeling I had after meeting him to leave. So, I did what I always do when I need to change the vibe: I turned on my camera and started recording another video.

CHAPTER 9
WHEN THE SKY TURNS PERSONAL
RIDGE

My favorite part of the job so far had to be the high-tech weather station that took up nearly a full wall of the cabin. There were several thermometers at high and low points of the area, a few wind gauges and even a webcam of the lake that all fed into this one machine.

Our biggest threat this time of year were microbursts. High pressure storm systems that moved in rapidly and did a lot of damage. I'd heard from Travis that just last year, dozens of trees were knocked down in a furious microburst on the other side of the lake shore.

This part of the Rockies was known for its wind. Growing up, we'd get windstorms that would last for days and make life almost impossible on the ranch. The hay would blow away, the fields would dry up no matter how much irrigation we'd have running and if it was winter, the snow would pile up anywhere it could. We'd have white sheaths covering the west facing windows entirely. But even in the midst of trials, life in the wild west was superior to anything else I could have imagined.

I'd take three feet of snow over three miles of a traffic jam anyway. I'd have rather sewn up my worn jeans than have a shopping mall or delivery truck at my fingertips. City life would kill me.

Life in the mountains was a fever dream. In the summer, I'd pick wild dandelions to brew for my coffee and sleep out under the stars. In the winter, after working the cows, I'd put my frozen stiff clothing next to the fireplace where it would stand up on its own. Some of my fondest memories involved lining up frozen clothes from my family.

Yes, I wouldn't and I couldn't trade this life for anything else. I thanked the Lord every day for placing me right where He did; I knew how fortunate I was to have been born here in the wilds instead of in a city. The only thing missing in my life was a wife.

Part of the reason I sought a break from the ranch was my desire to meet women. Not in a serial dating sort of manner; I'd seen my brother Patrick get a cell phone, upload his likeness to a dating app, and within the hour be trekking three hours to meet seven different women at the various coffee shops. Once, he got his messages mixed up and offered to take two of them to church on the same day, same building. Thankfully, they were understanding, but the problem was, he liked them both and couldn't choose. He'd never had much sense, so he told them that. Luckily, they chose for him, and then he had no lady to take with him to listen to the Word of the Lord that morning. That's what he got for trying to make a house of worship a dating scene. No, I wanted nothing of the sort.

    I'd always pictured myself meeting my wife in the place that I loved the most— outside. In nature. Where I'm the closest to the God that I serve, reveling in His creation. So, when I got the wild hair to apply to the ranger program last year, right after my twenty-fifth birthday, I considered the fact that I may just meet the woman that God has set aside for me, and the thought was exciting, but it didn't rule my life. I had a desire to marry and have a family of my own. I would have loved to see the world from the eyes of my children one day. But, if it was God's will that I didn't marry, I was okay with that, too. For now, I was just waiting to hear His voice to tell me which way to go.

God led me to Yellowstone. Ever since I was a kid, I enjoyed coming here. The whole family—my folks, my two brothers and I—would visit for a week every summer. It was always in the back of my mind—and heart—that I wanted to spend a summer here one day to fully explore its vast landscapes. From the mud pots that looked like they were out of a science fiction movie, to the rainbow geyser that was Grand Prismatic Spring, and all of the other hidden valleys, corners, and streams that may have been lesser known, but just as exciting.

Now, as I sat in the rickety log chair of the cabin that was hewn together from logs that had seen several generations of explorers in the very park I was blessed to be in, all I could think about was the woman with the purple tent.

Sure, she was rude to me, but she didn't owe me anything—we were strangers. She didn't know that I was not a threat to her. She was a woman, a very beautiful woman at that—seemingly traveling alone. If I had been her friend, I would have told her to be tough and standoffish to any man who came her way. The thought of being her friend sent adrenaline up my veins. Sure, she was a certain type of woman that probably wouldn't have meshed well with my outdoorsy lifestyle. But her femininity was striking. She looked like she would be a lot to handle, but I could handle a lot. I was as tough as they came.

"Ridge?" Travis came back through the door, bursting my thought bubble and actually startling me a little. I knocked over my coffee cup, which thankfully, was empty. "Didn't mean to scare you. I hope you didn't wet your pants," he said, pointing at my coffee cup that would have spilled its contents, if there were any.

"I'm fine. I was just deep in thought, that's all." *I'm going to have to get used to being interrupted out here in civilization.* I laughed at the thought, considering this was what most considered to be the complete opposite of civilization.

"Oh good. I hope you had a good think," he rolled his eyes. I was starting to think Travis was a real jerk.

"What's up?" I said, standing up from my chair. Usually, when I came face to face with a problem—let it be an animal or a man—things started to look differently. Travis, who had about twenty years on me, but I made up for it in size and height, shook his head.

"Nothing. I was just going to rant about that talk I just had to give. You wouldn't believe how only two people showed up, yet I had to still do the whole discussion. And did they have *questions."* He squeezed the bridge between his eyes. "You'd think it was some of these tourists' first day on earth. Like, why would you ask me, 'Is the lake fresh water or salt'? I'm talking about volcanoes."

"Probably because it's unusual that Yellowstone Lake is freshwater, considering most volcanic lakes tend to be acidic." I crossed my arms, not seeing his point.

"Oh, so we have a scholar? I forgot—where did you go to school?" He gave me a look that bordered on jealousy and evil.

"School of life. I've been coming here since I was just a little fella. In fact, I used to attend the talks on this lake, and they were taught by a very patient, knowledgeable ranger." That did it. Travis looked like he was going to blow his top. He left without a word, and I was thankful to once again be in the silence.

I was not one to complain. If I was, I'd have given Bob a call up in Montana and have seen about Travis finding some other rocks to kick. For now, I would pray to the God above that Travis' attitude would not interfere with my life. As I spoke to God, a wind gust came up that sounded so strong, it could have ripped the very roof over my head right off.

I jumped to the weather station on the other side of the small cabin. The gust took a moment to load; fifty-five miles an hour. Another one followed. *We are surely in micro-burst territory now*, I thought. If only Travis hadn't stormed out, he would be safe from this. Now, who knew what had happened to him? The sky darkened, bringing a loud, choppy rain with it. The wind howled; I pictured the little wooden shakes on the roof being gone when it was over. Then, I once again remembered the woman in the purple tent, and I jumped into action.

Running through the woods, it was all I could do to close the door of the station behind me. I didn't need that equipment to get wet or destroyed, but the Lord knew I would, if it meant I could save someone from harm. The short distance became longer when I was trying my hardest to get back. My belt was empty of the replacement bear spray I meant to grab in the station, and I prayed that I wouldn't need it as it sat over a hundred yards away, behind a closed door. But mostly, I prayed for the woman's safety.

When I reached her campsite, the trees were swaying back and forth like they were sitting on a Lazy Susan in my grandmother's kitchen cabinet. *My* tourist was nowhere to be found. Her things were scattered around, including a large bag of granola that had fallen from the tree we strung it up in. When I went to grab it before it got destroyed, the rain started hammering harder, and I heard a cry from inside the tent. Dropping the granola, I ran over to the thin, purple fabric that must have had a wind rating of five miles per hour by the way the fibers were already shredding.

CHAPTER 10
MEET CUTE, BUT MAKE IT A RESCUE
RIDGE

"Ma'am, are you in there?" The tent unzipped halfway before the zipper broke, and the woman ripped the rest of it open with little effort. She reached her hand out, just as a tree fell and landed right on her car, not even fifty yards from us, breaking all of the windshield and doors. The sound was startling enough that the woman sprung out of the tent and into my arms, as if to use my body to shield her own from danger. I didn't mind in the slightest, and thought that was a great idea, so I let her. Tree branches were blowing all around us, and I wrapped my arms around her petite frame to protect her from any harm that might come our way. In the midst of the violent snapping of trees and radical winds that took my ranger hat with them, I couldn't help but notice that she smelled like the wildflowers that grow in my favorite mountain meadows.

The storm ended as quickly as it started, but I held onto her a moment after while the sky cleared, just in case. At least, that's what I told myself, because now that I held her, I knew I wanted to hold her for the rest of my life, even if she was a jerk. I'd never felt more prepared for a challenge.

"Are you okay?" I asked, letting go of her slowly. She was shivering cold. We were both soaking wet, but her clothes were rapidly drying as the sun returned.

"I told you not to call me ma'am," she snarked with chattering teeth. Small pieces of her eyelashes began to fall as she let out a squeal.

"My apologies. Perhaps you could tell me your name, so I won't have to use that phrase by accident in your presence ever again?" She contemplated my question for a minute before standing up, suddenly free of the heavy fibers that lined her eyes before. Now, she looked even more beautiful.

"Ember." *Like embers to a blaze.* I knew there was a fire inside of this woman.

"Nice to meet you, Ember. I'm Ridge Sawyer. And I'm working with a cranky fellow ranger named Travis in that cabin right over there if you'd like to come inside and warm up. I have a small fireplace and a hot pot of coffee." She nodded almost immediately, before turning and looking at her car when she burst into tears, black mascara running down her face.

"What am I supposed to do now? I'm stuck here, in this stormy hellscape with no car, no food, and no cell phone service!" A smile cracked on my lips. It wasn't that I wanted to see her cry; in fact, that broke my heart. When that first tear rolled, I wanted to do anything I could to make sure I never saw another again. But I couldn't hold back my smile, and she noticed fast. I had a feeling this woman didn't miss a thing.

"And just what is so funny?" She crossed her arms, her chin still quivering.

"Nothing, ma—, I mean, Ember. It's just that, other than the food part, and I'm very sorry about your vehicle—you've just described my *dreamscape.*"

"Just what is so dreamy about this situation?" She stomped her foot in protest as she shivered.

"Here, let's get warmed up. I'll tell you all about it later," I said, wanting more than anything to put my arm around her in a gentlemanly way, but respecting her boundaries, too.

"Wha—what was that?" she asked as we started on foot towards my station.

"That was a microburst. A very fast-moving storm system that can fell just about any tree around us, like it did. I'm very sorry it happened." And I was sorry. This poor woman came here so ill-prepared and was chewed up and spit out by nature within the hour of her arrival. "Thankfully, the only casualty is your car."

"And my granola. And my phone." She held up a waterlogged device with a cracked screen that she'd been gripping onto this whole time as the tears started falling again.

"Don't cry, Ember. Those things are a dime a dozen."

"I know. I just feel like this was all a giant mistake."

"How so? What was your plan?" I couldn't wait to hear what she said.

"I mean, I didn't really have one. I just bought the tent yesterday at an outdoor clearance sale. It was only thirty-three dollars, and it felt like the stars were aligning for me to take an adventure." As we reached the ranger station, I could hear her shoes squishing with water. She'd gotten hit more with rain than I realized.

"I don't know about the stars, but I do know that God makes good of situations for those who follow Him." She stared at me like I was an alien from outer space for a moment, before her expressions softened.

"You're right," she said, sniffling again. "I've gotten so far off track of what I am supposed to be doing. My best friend says I'm addicted to my phone. I've been trying to get brand deals to promote items to my followers and this was my first paying gig for this outfit." It was as if her tears had been turned on like a well pump and now it needed two people to turn it off.

"Those are pretty good hiking clothes, I'd say. And if you ask me, this right here would make a pretty great ad," I said, causing her tears to stop. She looked up at me and laughed; the most joyous sound I'd ever heard. One day, I imagined it would compare to the angels singing in heaven.

"That's the most ridiculous thing I've ever heard," and just like that, she was rude again. I smiled defiantly.

"Why's that?"

"Because. This isn't about hiking. This is about looking good in the clothes. Posing. Setting a scene. No one cares if the clothes or products or whatever item it is works or is worth its weight. They just buy based on the aesthetic. *The vibe*." I wanted to tell her that was the most ridiculous thing that *I ever heard,* but I held my tongue. I could spar with this woman, really go toe to toe, but she'd been through quite a bit in the last ten minutes, and for all I knew, she wasn't thinking clearly. Then again, it might have been fun.

"That's the most ridiculous thing *I've* ever heard," I said with a tone of playfulness. She took the bait.

"Oh yeah, park ranger boy?" Ember grabbed the coat hanging on the hook by the door—my coat—and put it on. She was swimming in it, and it came to her thigh. She stomped over to the fireplace and put her hands out, soaking up the heat. I waited for her next comment—the conclusion to her comeback—but it didn't come. I poured her a cup of coffee while we stood in silence.

"How do you take your coffee?" I asked, holding a steaming cup.

"Hot," she said, reaching out and taking a big swig. The look of repulsion on her face made me smirk. "Though, I wouldn't call *this* coffee."

"Yeah, it's not too fancy up here in my neck of the woods."

"I mean, I drink it black. I'm not some boujee coffee girl, despite what some would believe." She rolled her eyes. "I'm tough. I can handle it. It's just not Arabica coffee. And I have a sneaking suspicion, it's not organic, either." She took another sip from the mug, trying her hardest to give me a stoic expression as she drank it.

"Had I known I was going to have company, I would have made a pour over with my French roast." Her eyes widened and she *almost* smiled.

CHAPTER 11
THE HOTTEST MAN WITH THE LEAST WI-FI
EMBER

I can't believe I was a damsel in distress, not even an hour after I met this infuriatingly gorgeous man who ruffled all the feathers I didn't even know I had. The way he looked at me—so raw, so real—like I'd never truly been seen before. I'd only ever been seen as the perfectly curated image I portrayed online. And Ridge? Well, he saw right through that facade. I thought that's why he bothered me so much. But the storm made the situation dire—when I needed help, I called out, and he was there.

It all happened so fast. I was taking some selfies. Considering pulling down my big bag of granola for a snack. I was craving some chocolate. About to take a short nap in my cute purple tent that looked so *aesthetic* in this moody, wilderness setting. Sure, it wasn't as sturdy as I thought. The carpet in my hotel room last night made it seem a little sturdier than it was, but, what could go wrong?

I noticed the sky was darkening, but I just assumed the sun set early here in the woods. Like, really early. It wasn't even dinner time yet, though, and I still had some freezer dried food in my car. I wondered if those needed to be kept from bears, too, but I just couldn't imagine a grizzly having any desire to eat something that needed to be reconstituted first. Unless he caught it like a fish and took it over to that giant lake, it would just be like eating chalk. Nah, the food was fine, I decided. But then, the gust of wind came. It happened so fast, I felt like I had whiplash. I dove into my tent for cover, thinking something might fly into me like a hubcap or a roof shingle, like this was some setting straight out of Oz.

The wind only got worse. The only thing holding the tent down was my weight. I guess I didn't do that great of a job anchoring it down after all. Fear ran through my veins— was this a hurricane? Did they get tornadoes up here? It was just me and my thoughts, which were filled with regret. The only distraction was the storm overhead. And for the first time in my life, I cried out to God for protection, and then I heard a voice. But it wasn't the one I was expecting.

"Ma'am, are you in there?" Since I doubted that God would call me ma'am, it meant that someone was here to help!

Except this time, I'd never been so happy to be called ma'am in my life. When I tried to unzip the tent, the zipper broke off in my hands. *Now I know why it was on sale.* Then, the noise came: A tree groaned as it gave up its roots, followed by glass shattering and metal crushing. I sprung out of the tent and into the man's chest for protection, unable to ignore that his body felt like it was made of steel. As if he was the strongest man on earth. He responded to my running into him by wrapping his thick biceps around me. Normally, I would have felt the need to object. To tell him to hold his horses—I don't let anyone touch me. I don't even hug my family. But the moment I ran into him, my walls started to fall down as the world collapsed around me, and I felt true masculinity exude from this body melted to mine. In the midst of danger... he made me feel safe.

As we crouched down, he leaned over me, shielding me from the heavy sheets of rain. At one point, my ponytail was straight in the air from the pressure swirling all around us. I would have laughed if it didn't seem so dire. I would have made a snarky comment if I thought I was going to live to see another day. But then, it stopped. Just as fast as it started. As if the wind took its last breath before inhaling the rain cloud that showered over us.

The man I refused to look at slowly released me from our embrace, and I felt my body heat escaping as he took his arms away. Though I would never admit it, I liked the feeling of being in his arms, and I was disappointed when he took them away.

Then, the questions started. Was I okay? What was my name? *Dude, read a room.* I was not okay, and he called me ma'am. Again. I felt like a drowned rat, and I couldn't imagine I looked that much better than one. I didn't have much preparation for any of it, let alone seeing the wreckage of what was left. My tent, gone. My food, washed away. Little bits of granola were spread around me like ashes in a fire. My eyelash extensions, which were already on their last leg, past expiry, came out in clumps. Then, I saw the remains of my car, and I couldn't hold back my tears. On top of it all, my phone was toast. Waterlogged. The crack had grown larger during the event, and the screen had water below it. My hand hurt from gripping it as hard as I did through the event. I held it harder than anything else, but it still got destroyed.

Ridge was an intriguing name for this guy, whose muscles were now highlighted through his drenched clothes that stuck to him as if he was dipped in paint. After leading me into safety, and a tragic excuse for a cup of coffee, I sat by the crackling fire and took it upon myself to use someone's jacket as an emergency blanket. I didn't know whose jacket it was, but it smelled like pine needles and musk. Nature's natural cologne, and I didn't hate it. I wondered if it belonged to his grumpy co-worker, Travis, whom he told me about. Perhaps he was even hotter than Ridge and wouldn't look right through me? But the second I started getting my hopes up that Travis was going to be the man to get me away from Ridge, the door opened.

"Hey, Travis," Ridge's deep voice barked from the other side of the log ranger station. I turned my head, eyeing him expectantly, letting out a sigh almost immediately. Not only was he twice my age—maybe even triple—he was half the stature of Ridge. Realizing that this jacket I was enjoying the pleasantries of most definitely belonged to the man I was taking my anger out on was humbling.

"Who's this?" Travis asked Ridge, as if I couldn't see, hear, or speak for myself. To be fair, I hadn't seen my reflection post-storm. Microburst. Whatever it was called.

"This is Ember. She was camped over yonder, and a microburst came through. A ponderosa pine tree took out her whole camp." Ridge spoke matter-of-factly.

"And my car," I piped up, but Travis turned and rolled his eyes. Ridge was right—this guy was rude.

"Now what are you going to do with her? We don't make a practice of taking inexperienced tourists on. No matter how cute you think they are." Travis spoke defiantly, and Ridge shook his head and stood.

"I don't need your permission to help someone," Ridge said. His body made it obvious that he could lift Travis' entire being with one arm. Travis, not backing down, just stood there. Though from this angle, it looked like his feet were begging to take a step back. "Is there anything else that you need?" Ridge stood, arms to his side. I crossed mine in my own defense. Travis finally relented, putting his hands up in the air.

"No. I'll leave you to it. Good luck with that," he said, walking out the door and not closing it all the way behind him.

"What a jerk," I said. Ridge nodded and closed the door behind Travis.

"He's very unhappy in his aimless, Godless existence. I'm praying for him every day." Ridge spoke about God so fluidly. I'd never been around a man like that before. Some of the guys on social media, like Graham Jones, posted Bible verses in captions. I wondered if they also spoke this way? For some reason, I'd bet that they didn't. Maybe it was all for show. The thought crossed my mind that I was also living for show, but before I could think any further, I remembered my phone.

"Do you have a bag of rice?" I held it up with a pout on my tear-stained face.

"I'm afraid not," he said with a shrug. "But if you're hungry, I have some chili that I can put on the stove." He held up a round thermos, my stomach growling at the thought of it, but I couldn't let this go just yet.

"No, I mean—yes, chili—but the rice is for my phone." He gave me a confused expression. Oh my goodness—was this guy *living under a rock?* Did he not know what rice was for in this situation? "If your phone gets waterlogged, like mine here—" I held it up, my mental health shattering by the second as my emotions stayed right behind each word, threatening to make tears again—"you drop it in rice, and it absorbs everything. Sometimes, the phone will work again." Ridge nodded.

"There's no cell service out here. At least for fifty miles. You are welcome to use my phone. I also have a satellite phone if you want to go outside to use it. I can also step out if you need some privacy." He held up a brick of a device and motioned to the outside, and to the wall phone. He was generous with his options.

"I don't think I need to go back out there anytime soon," I huffed. *Great.* No car, no phone. Ridge walked over to the stove and put the chili on. It was only a few seconds before the intoxicating aroma of spices filled the room.

CHAPTER 12
THE PARK DOES NOT CARE ABOUT MY AESTHETIC
EMBER

I watched Ridge move throughout the room. This man had confidence in him, a masculinity that seemed to be extinct. Nowadays, people said that masculinity was a bad thing. Harmful to society. But this was what men were supposed to be. Strong. Protectors. Safety in a storm, metaphorically and real. As I considered what it was about him that irked me, I realized it was the same feeling I had when Traci commented about my phone use and the way I dressed. Add Ridge to the list of things that made me feel uncomfortable. Unchartered. Untethered. Lost in the wilderness.

Sure, I'd hidden behind a lot of things in my life. My clothes, my online persona. But everyone did that. No one was really who they said they were online. I looked at my phone again instinctively, trying the buttons for the one hundredth time, in case that God performed some miracle and now it would work.

It didn't. *Who was I without all of this?* The thought spread through my mind like a wildfire.

"Here you go." He handed me the bottom bowl that unscrewed from his thermos, an army green color that really gave off that camping vibe. Complete with a black metal spoon.

"Very *aesthetic,*" I commented, looking at the beautiful meal presentation with my backdrop of the fireplace. I checked my phone once more. It was a shame I wouldn't be able to take a photo of this. "You don't happen to have a camera, do you, ranger boy?" He laughed and rubbed his forehead and then ran his hand through his lustrous, dark hair that went just past his ears.

"I have an old-fashioned one," he said. "But that chili looks better than it tastes, and the more it cools off, the worse that's going to be." I took heed to his warning and took a small bite, blowing on it as the steam from the bowl let me know it was going to be a scorcher.

The aromas of spices, ranging from chili powder, garlic, and a hint of sweetness from brown sugar, invaded all of my senses. Hearty meat commingled with soft sweet potatoes and bell peppers in a rustic dance of flavors. It was the ultimate comfort food and with every bite, my body warmed several degrees.

"This is amazing," I said, and within seconds I was taking several more bites.

"Now I know you're starving," he smiled, sitting back down at his desk.

"I mean it. I normally don't like chili because I'm not a huge bean lover," I said through my chewing.

"Real chili doesn't have beans. It's got meat and potatoes," he nodded in agreement. "Is this your first time having bison?" I stopped in my tracks, looking down at the food in my bowl.

"What do you mean, 'is this'? As in, this isn't beef?" I felt panic. I thought for a moment about it. Did I have a problem with meat that wasn't beef? No, probably not, depending on where it was sourced, that is. But it *was* one of those things that I would have liked to have known ahead of time.

"Nope. That's bison. We raise it on my family's ranch up North. Pretty big operation. We have some cattle, some bison. My brother even has some llamas." He put his gorgeous hair behind his ear. There was something captivating about seeing this guy move.

"Don't tell me you eat the llamas, too," I said, taking another bite and analyzing the flavors, realizing that it tasted very similar to beef, and I continued devouring the bowl.

"He uses them as pack animals. Kind of fun, actually. There's nothing like taking llamas into the mountains like I'm a sherpa from the Himalayas." A smile formed across my lips before I could properly restrain myself. I glanced up at Ridge, taking in his extraordinarily handsome face, and it was too late. He saw me. "There we go. Should I tell you more about the llamas, to cheer you up? Or, I could tell you about the chickens my mother raises. It's quite the zoo." I admired his stamina in this conversation, but I didn't know how much more animal talk I had in me, as I felt the reality set in for my situation. Tears formed in the corners of my eyes.

"I need to make a call," I said, setting down the bowl and choking back hysteria. His eyes grew wide, turning from me and immediately grabbing the phone and handing it to me.

"I'll step outside. Take your time," he said, as he quickly slipped out the door, shutting it behind him. Truthfully, it felt good just to be alone for a moment. I spent quite a lot of time alone these days, surfing social media, connecting with followers virtually. The thoughts started pouring in; if my phone was working, maybe one of my followers could help me? If my phone was working, I could post the photos I took and keep my one and only brand deal intact. I looked down at my clothes as I contemplated my phone call like I was standing in a holding cell, and it was the only one I was going to get. Ridge was right; this would make a good ad. But I wasn't ready for that kind of humiliation. The brand was looking for aesthetics, not a real near-death experience. At least, not for my debut into brand deals.

I only knew two phone numbers by heart—my mother and Traci. I had already checked in with my mother and if I called her right now, she'd flip out. As I weighed my options, I decided it might have been nice if the National Guard would have been called to come rescue me. Perhaps Ridge could have filmed my ascent into a helicopter. Ugh. If only he'd had a smartphone. I dialed Traci and held my breath as I knew she didn't like to answer phone numbers she didn't know.

"Hello?" Her voice on the other end sounded small. Tired. Weary. Could she have been sitting around, worried about me?

"Traci, it's me, Ember. My phone isn't working and—" I was cut off.

"Hello? Hellooooo?" she kept repeating, before the line went dead. *Great.* What was the point of a phone if it didn't work?

"That's it!" I shouted, nearly throwing the phone down. Ridge, standing on the porch, heard my voice and turned around. "Your phone doesn't work, buddy!" As soon as the words came out of my mouth, I realized just how *unbecoming* it was of me to have had a meltdown. He cautiously walked inside.

"It's not working?" he said, carefully speaking each syllable.

"No, it's not. They can't hear me on the other line," I whispered, trying to regain some sense of control over myself.

"Hmm. Oh, here you go. It wasn't plugged in all the way. I'm sorry; this technology is terrible. It will call out, but they can't hear you. Want to give it another try?" he asked, handing me back the phone as he checked all of the cords and outlets. I shrugged, as a fleeting question crossed my mind: What could come of me getting Traci worried? Ultimately, I decided it was better to let her know than my mom.

"Yes. Thank you," I said, as I waited expectantly for him to return to the outside porch. But he did me one better, grabbing his keys off the desk.

"I'm just going to run a quick errand while you make your phone calls. I only have enough water for one person here, and there's another small station up the road that I can take supplies from. Will you be okay for say, an hour?" My heartbeat quickened.

"Yes, I think I'll manage." My tone was just getting more bitter by the moment, and I was filled with regret. Ridge nodded, surely hoping my attitude would have been adjusted by the time he returned. The moment the door closed behind him, I let out my breath. *God, why am I so rude?* The words stunned me. It had been a long time since I had started any sort of dialogue with God, although this did seem like the right time to do so.

I didn't dwell on the thoughts for more than I had to, as I was already redialing Traci. This time, the phone rang five times before she answered, and I immediately started talking.

"Traci! It's Ember," I said in a shout.

"Ember? Are you okay?" Her voice still sounded very off.

"No, I'm trapped in Yellowstone! A storm came through, and a tree fell on my car!" The tears came like someone flipped a switch. Traci listened to the story, making a few gasp noises here and there.

"I'm so sorry, Ember. Do you want me to call your mom? Or, are you going to call her next?" A pit formed in my stomach.

"I guess I was hoping that you would come get me," I said, sheepishly.

"In Yellowstone? Ember, I can't do that. I'm sorry. My grandma is back in the hospital. I'm actually sitting in the waiting room right now as she's getting checked out by her doctors." Guilt washed over me. I knew something was wrong with Traci, but I hadn't asked what. *God, why am I such a terrible friend?* Despite the realization that I was a jerk, I couldn't stop now. I'd come way too far in my self-centered journey.

"What about like, after? I mean, my mom will kill me if she hears about this, and..." My voice trailed off.

"After *what,* Ember?" I struggled to answer the question.

"I'm sorry; I didn't mean like *that...*"

"Call your mom." Traci's voice sounded like tears of her own were coming soon. We both stayed on the line for a few moments, hesitating, and I listened to her breathing. There was a lot I wished I knew how to say to my longest friend; the only person in my life, whom I didn't share blood with, stood by my side faithfully. I could feel that I was finally losing her, too, pushing her away from me, as I had done with everyone else in my life. But it wasn't really me. It was the persona I'd created and for the thousandth time in the last 48 hours, I felt extremely uncomfortable by a thought. Traci whispered something I couldn't quite make out, as I was lost in my own problematic thoughts, and hung up. The dial tone was deafening. I turned off the phone.

Minutes had passed since Ridge's departure. I had already decided I didn't want to call my mom and face the wrath of my decisions—my parents had co-signed on my car. My dad had joked about me taking care of this car, because it was the last time they were going to help me.

See, there had been a few other mistakes made in my history. I guess you could say that it was a bit of a pattern for me, if you looked at it the way my parents did, but in my opinion, they were all incidents out of my control. Like what happened here today: I didn't make that tree fall on it. That tree had been standing for hundreds of years. Why would it choose to come down today, on my Subaru? Sure, my last car had been stolen and vandalized because I forgot to lock it. They found it gutted by the river, under a bridge. The car before that had the engine go out after I forgot to get the oil change done for a long time. Before that, well, it was a stick shift. I didn't know it was going to lurch forward and hit that car in front of me.

    As I weighed my options, I considered that maybe this time, it was at least partially my fault.

CHAPTER 13
THE STORM WASN'T THE ONLY PROBLEM
RIDGE

Ember was like my grandma's senior chihuahua, Frannie. Cute as a button; just seeing her, you'd think, 'I'd like to cuddle with her', but the moment you got close- it was like she was doing her tryouts for a *Jaws* sequel.

A deep, guttural growl would come from her small, frail body that looked like it wouldn't survive sixty seconds in the wild. She donned a pink coat and painted nails that my grandma insisted were done by the groomer as part of the package deal. Frannie looked like a princess that needed protecting from the elements, and something inside of me wanted to be that protector. Much like Ember in that way, too.

My grandma would make excuses for her. "She's just feeling extra spicy today," or, "she's not used to being around men." The comparison was unbelievably humorous. I still haven't given up on Frannie. Last Christmas, she sniffed my sock and then instead of peeing on it, she sat near me. As in, within a few yards. We were all amazed that my persistence of winning the heart of this seemingly soul-less dog was starting to pay off. And, like Frannie, I wanted to do the same with Ember. I wanted to win her over.

It's not that I want to be treated poorly; I just like a challenge. It's who I am. It's in my DNA. I come from a very rugged terrain near the Canadian border that if you get turned around in a blizzard, you might just freeze to death before you find your footing again. That's how I grew up. Nothing came easy. And I liked that. I wanted to earn everything I had.

The only thing I didn't have to earn was my salvation in Christ. He washed me anew and now I am as pure as the snowfall that usually comes up to my neck every fall, winter and spring. God knows the number of hairs on my head and He also knows just the kind of woman I am looking for- one that doesn't let me have the keys to the kingdom right off the bat. A woman I could work for.

When I reached the ranger station, I thought of just how upset she acted about the phone not working. Like Frannie, Ember is used to a certain standard of living. Of communication. It seems very important to her to be able to stay in contact with her people. I wondered if she was close with her family. Does she have siblings? Where does she come from? What does she do? I couldn't wait to find out.

I retrieved extra supplies, loading them up in the pickup truck and heading back down the road. The thought crossed my mind:

would Ember still be there when I returned? As if she was a scared cat- would she try to flee on foot? I sure hoped not, as I looked out at the once again darkening sky, that was hinting at trouble ahead.

Back at my station, I breathed a sigh of relief when I saw Ember inside. She was still sitting in the same spot by the fire, and still wearing my coat. It looked good on her. I unloaded the case of water and carried it under one arm, opening the door with another. Ember was on the phone, and I didn't want to invade her privacy. So, I set the water down and made my way out, but not before hearing some of the conversation.

"I'm doing good. It's really pretty here. I have a camp near the lake, a pretty purple tent, and I've already met the rangers that are stationed nearby." What a way to spin it. Maybe she's an optimist after all?

I return back outside, giving her some space to make all of the exaggerations she needs to without my judgement. Out on the porch, overlooking Yellowstone Lake, my thoughts usually consist of the Supervolcano that is sitting under this enormous body of water. I always enjoy considering God's amazing design of this geological wonder of a park, but today, my thoughts are robbed of anything nature related and replaced by the blonde haired, green eyed woman with perfectly painted artificial nails that is sitting by the fire and wearing my coat.

"I'm all done," she hollers out to me, and I look back in the ranger station to see her staring into the fire. I walk in, hesitantly, like I would approach Frannie.

"Do you want some water?" I ask, pointing to the case I just brought from the other station. She nods, and I hand her a bottle. "So..." I started off, wanting to ask if she got what she needed out of those phone conversations that we both knew was a total lie, but I didn't know where to begin.

"That was my mother," she said, pulling the coat around her as tight as it would go. "If she knew the truth, the Coast Guard would be swimming up in a matter of seconds." I shrugged.

"Maybe that wouldn't be such a bad thing," I said, not knowing her plans here, but also realizing I did not want her to leave.

"Oh, it would be the worst thing to ever happen to me. Trust me. I may be twenty-four years old, but I'd be grounded for the rest of my life," she said, squeezing the bridge of her nose for dramatic effect.

"She must care a lot about you," I said, and in turn, Ember shrugged.

"I guess she does, yeah."

"Family is everything to me," I offered up in conversation. Ember just kept staring at the fireplace, and I took a seat at my desk chair, feeling the warmth of the cracking wood radiate throughout.

"Oh no!" She yells, catching me off guard with her outburst. I stand and turn to her. "Where am I going to sleep tonight? You said that the lodges don't even open for another few weeks!" Now this is a problem I could solve.

"You can sleep in my cabin," I said, so proudly that I was sure she was going to get up and hug me with her overwhelming gratitude. Instead, I was met with such a fierce look of anger that I wiggled my fingers and toes just to ensure I hadn't been turned to stone.

"Ha-ha! Yeah right, buddy! Is this what you think this is?" She motioned between us with her hands. "I don't know what kind of girl you think I am, but you've got me all wrong." My cheeks reddened when I realized the implications of my suggestions that she *thought* I made.

"No, I didn't mean it like that, Ember. I'm sorry, but please take my word for it, that I would never..." I trailed off. She doesn't know me, and explaining things to this type of hard shell of a woman was not going to earn her trust. Like Frannie, that would only come with my actions and persistence. "I will sleep elsewhere. You may sleep in my living quarters that have an old fashioned wood slab for an inside lock on the door." Her face looked at me for a moment, she was still noticeably angry, but that anger had started to thaw out slowly.

"Thank you," she said, softly. "I really appreciate your kindness."

"You're welcome, darlin'." I tipped my cowboy hat at her, thankful it was back on my head and my hat that went with my uniform had blown away in the storm. I didn't care much for that one. Her cheeks were gaining more of a rosy glow as she warmed by the fire.

"Where will you sleep?" The question from her perfectly pouty lips came several minutes after it was decided that she would take my bed, and seemingly, out of nowhere. Still, I was happy to answer any questions she had for me.

"Outside."

CHAPTER 14
CITY GIRL, REAL TROUBLE
RIDGE

"Outside!? In this?" Ember stood and went to the window, watching the breeze blow around and rustle the trees up. "It's an absolute hurricane out there!" I laughed, which I could immediately tell by the look on her face that laughter was not the response she wanted.

"This isn't nothin'. It's only blowing twenty miles per hour. You saw for yourself what can happen out here and that isn't supposed to happen again tonight, so don't worry about me." While she didn't have the look of worry per se, she looked extremely put out by my sleeping outside, which I didn't know how to take. Was she not wanting me to rough it, in a sweet way, because maybe she thought she might like me? Or, did she think I couldn't handle the balmy temperatures that it dipped to out here at night, and this was more of an insult?

"I just think it's crazy for you to do that," she shrugged.

"May I remind you that you, yourself, were going to sleep outside tonight, if it hadn't been for that microburst coming through and destroying all of your belongings?" She rolled her eyes and crossed her arms.

"Yeah, I guess you're right. At least I had my car so I could sleep in it if I needed to." She shook her head.

"And I have my truck. But I won't need it. I have a sleeping bag rated for subzero temperatures that I've personally tested out in weather way worse than this, along with an affinity for sleeping out under the stars."

"What about bears? Won't they just come and like, kill you or something?" Her question, paired with the most serious look I thought I'd ever seen on someone's face, made me bust up and laugh.

"Bears are absolutely a threat, but I have nothing to attract them. No food on me, and I won't be threatening their young. Besides, I will sleep in the bed of my truck, not the ground where they might decide to just walk over me at night. And I'll keep the fire outside going while I sleep. Bears don't usually run towards fire." She nodded, appearing to like this answer.

"Okay, then. It's settled. You sleep outside and I'll sleep in your cabin. I'm getting out of here as soon as I can. In fact, I better call a tow truck. Do you have one of those phone books laying around by chance?"

"Good idea. I bet you get some nice scrap metal prices for that rig," I said, turning to the computer and opening an internet browser.

"Scrap metal?" she asked, looking back at me, then suddenly standing up, her eyes narrowing past me. "Do you have the internet on that computer?"

"Yeah, of course we do. I'm actually tracking a wolf—" She cut me off, suddenly appearing directly behind me.

"May I uh... check my emails?" I stood up, waving her into the chair that she sat down in immediately. Her fingers were furiously typing away for a few seconds and the next thing I knew, a big colorful screen appeared with her gorgeous face on it. "Hi, I'm Ember," it read. She was smiling in her photo, with a beautiful, glamorous setting. I realized this woman and I were from two different worlds entirely, and yet, God crossed her path with mine. *Lord, is this woman the one for me or is this a lesson to be learned for one of us?* I walked away from the computer, giving her some privacy as I pondered my prayers.

I sat with my back to the desk at the fire, and with every breath, I was waiting to hear what God had to say to me through this experience. But all I could hear was Ember scrolling with the little circular thing on the mouse. She wasn't typing, not clicking. Just a long, never-ending scroll. I checked my watch. Technically, I needed to log some reports. I especially needed to write down the day's happenings with the microburst that came through here. But no one was going to see that today, anyway. My boss in Montana had already gone home for the day, or had fallen asleep at his desk, which I heard was a common occurrence. That was a reason I knew this was the right position, because he was not the type to micromanage every move I made. As long as I got the work I needed to get done in a reasonable time frame, he would be happy with me, I'd heard. And out here, the job scope was so little on the computer. Most of it was outside in this great, big, beautiful haven that God created. Yellowstone filled me with wonder just thinking about it.

The warmth of the fire started to lull me into a sleepy feeling, and I dozed off for an undetermined amount of time. When I opened my eyes, the sky was almost completely dark, and I realized much time had passed since I let Ember use the computer. I stood up and turned, seeing she was still in the exact same spot and on the same website by the looks of it.

"I'm ready to call it for the day. Are you ready to go?"

"Oh, um... Just a minute." She started scrolling faster, as if she was looking for something. Then, she typed a few things, scrolled again, and ultimately let out a loud sigh. "I mean, I guess." Clicking around in the corner of the website, she signed out and grudgingly stood up. The clock above the computer said it was nearly seven in the evening. I was asleep for hours, and yet I felt more tired now.

Ember walked over to the coat rack and started to remove my jacket and hang it back on the hook where she found it.

"Keep the coat," I said firmly.

"No, that's okay. I don't want to risk losing followers if someone sees me in this thing." It took everything I had not to roll my eyes and laugh.

"And how would your *followers* see you?

"There's a live webcam right out here on the shore. You didn't tell me that I could livestream straight from the park! I am thinking I could host an update for them at that spot, tomorrow."

She seemed so proud of herself, I barely had the nerve to break the news to her.

"That webcam is mounted up on the roof. You'd have to climb up there in order to do so. Besides, it has a bit of a lag, being in the middle of nowhere, and all." There she went squeezing the bridge of her nose again.

"Okay, well, I'll figure something else out. Tomorrow, I'll just delete that announcement. I guess I really didn't think that one through," she said with a laugh. Her mood had noticeably improved during my snooze by the fire. Maybe she took a nap, too, I thought, but realized it had more to do with the internet than anything else.

"Alright then," I said, opening the door of my truck for her to climb in. She stood there for a moment with hesitancy. "Are you okay?"

"I don't have any other clothes to change into. Do you think that I could access anything in my car?"

"Ember, your car is flattened. We couldn't reach a bag inside if our arms had the radius of a toothpick." She slowly nodded, coming to the realization that all was lost.

"Okay," she said, climbing into the truck. I shut the door behind her.

When I got into the driver's seat, the intoxicating scent of her filled the car. It was like lavender and lilacs. Maybe it was her shampoo. Maybe it was God associating her to my most favorite places where I feltl the closest to Him. I didn't know for sure. But I couldn't wait to find out.

As we turned onto the main road out of the station, Ember's tanned and perfectly polished fingers reached for the radio. A preacher that I liked to listen to came on. His show was normally on much earlier, so I was surprised to hear it. Ember immediately started scanning the channels.

Finally landing on the one music station we got out here, picked up from Idaho, a country music crooner filled the truck. She turned it up. It wasn't two seconds later that I pulled into the parking spot.

"Home sweet home," I said, jumping out of the truck and walking around to get to her door. She was still unbuckling when I opened her door.

"You're quite the gentlemen, aren't you?" she said, but she didn't smile. It seemed to annoy her.

"This is the bare minimum of what a man should do for a woman. Any woman, that is. Mothers. Grandmas. Heck, if I had a little sister, I'd be doing this, too. Any man who can't open a door for a woman is just lazy." She didn't reply as we walked up to the small living quarters.

"Are you sure about this?" Ember pulled her jacket around her body like it was a shawl, feeling the chill in the air. Honestly, the air felt great to me. I loved to hear the howling of the wolves and coyotes. To feel the changes in the wind bringing different scents in all directions, from sage brush to sea water from the lake. And most of all, I loved stargazing. Waking up to birds chirping was just the icing on the cake. But I didn't tell her any of this.

"I'm sure. Let me get the fire going for you and then I'll leave," I said, opening the door for her. It was spotless inside, just how I had left it this morning. My father had been raised by a military general, and he passed on the wisdom of making one's bed first thing in the morning. I had taken it a step further and always tidied up after myself right away, so I would never have to revisit a mess. It worked wonders for the order in my life, but this experience tonight was the first time someone else was going to be added into the mix of my life.

Putting a few logs on, the flames were roaring in no time. I showed her where everything was and quickly brushed my teeth before heading towards the door.

"Will you sleep outside of here? Or, are you leaving?" Her voice was hesitant. Almost like a twinge of fear to it.

"I'll be right outside here, in the back of my truck. Do you see how this lock works?" I thought it might bring her comfort to know that no one could get in, if that's what she was concerned about. She nodded as I showed her.

"Thank you, Ridge. I mean it. This is so kind of you." Her voice had a childlike tone to it.

"It's my pleasure, Ember." I grabbed my sleeping bag that sat next to the door. I was always ready for an adventure. Ember walked around the cabin, eyes full of wonder. There wasn't much to see, but as she looked around, I saw things with fresh eyes. The old snowshoes hanging from a rusty nail on the wall. I couldn't wait to try those out. A large typography map of the park was tacked to the log wall above a small makeshift dining table. A tiny bathroom that had less square footage than a boat or an airplane lavatory. Lastly, a hearth for fires. The whole footprint could be walked in a handful of seconds for Ember, and even less for me with my being taller. But honestly, I loved this cabin. It had everything I could ever need while I was out here on this assignment, and seeing Ember in it brought up a fire in me that I didn't know how to extinguish. "Goodnight, then." I tipped my hat and closed the door behind me.

As I walked back to my truck, I prayed hard. *Lord, I'm feeling temptations towards her that I don't know how to navigate. Please keep my thoughts and heart pure around this woman.*

Rolling out my sleeping bag in my truck bed, I considered the woman who was just feet from me. Did I like her because she was gorgeous? Or, was there truly something more to this soul? Yes, she was rude. My word—was she also stunning to look at. But there was something else there. Beyond the facade that she was putting on that she was this perfectly kept internet superstar. There was a yearning in her to be seen and to be loved. And I recognized that the moment I saw her, because my heart mirrored the same desires.

It may have been an uphill battle that I didn't understand, but now, as I lay under the stars staring up at the beauty of God's creation, I could hear Him loud and clear. My soul recognized Ember the moment our eyes met earlier today. Something had happened here. And it certainly sounded crazy—heck, it felt crazy. But this woman was going to be something very important in my life, and I prayed that she felt it, too.

CHAPTER 15
MUSCLES FOR DAYS, CELL PHONE FOR NONE
EMBER

So many things had transpired in a short amount of time today. My car got smashed by a tree. My tent was destroyed. I lost all of my belongings and my phone—the lifeline of my existence—was broken.

Then, Traci. I regretted that phone call completely, but I didn't know she was in the hospital waiting room. Had my phone been working, I could have at least traced her location prior to calling.

Then, my mom. I decided to check in with her or risk a search party either way. I had to tell her that all was well even though it couldn't have been further from the truth of this reality.

Finally, Ridge. What was this guy's deal? He was all gentlemanly, opening doors, feeding me, and letting me sleep in his cabin. Actually, the cabin was amazing. I wished I could have posted about it. It was *so* aesthetic in a rustic sort of way. People would have eaten this up. Like I ate that amazing chili of his.

The computer! Knowing there was a place I could at least check my sites, which was the bare minimum, was a relief. Who knew the ranger station was akin to an internet cafe? Without the fancy coffee, of course. Yuck. But checking said socials today was admittedly a bit of a letdown. I went off the grid—literally—for nearly a full day and not one person noticed? I usually posted three times a day or more. An absence of posts didn't seem peculiar to a single one of my fifteen-thousand followers? And on top of that, nothing new or exciting was really happening. Nicollete was still in Africa, but was posting food pics. I was sure poolside bikini pictures would be coming tomorrow. Ugh, that reminded me. I had no other clothes than what was on my back, and this had to be the worst outfit to be stranded in!

Now, with the roaring fire bringing warmth to my bones, I removed the jacket I took from Ridge's ranger station. Hanging it up by the door, I saw that there was a name embroidered on the front, *Ridge.* My sneaking suspicion was right, and I had been wearing his coat all along.

After getting the last of my makeup off of my face, including the black smears that I'd been walking around with all day, and swishing toothpaste around in my mouth since I' had no toothbrush, I paced around the cabin for a while. My entire being felt restless.

My nighttime ritual had never been this simple. First, I did skincare for at least thirty minutes. I had a miniature skincare fridge on my makeup vanity where I kept my creams and serums. Once my makeup was washed off and my skin cleansed, I applied all of my balms and miracles, when I then put on my red light therapy face mask. I did that in bed, while scrolling my phone for the night. My bed at home had a pillow top that felt luxurious and like I was sleeping on a cloud. I used sound machines or had the television on to fall asleep. A humidifier ran in the background. And often, I fell asleep with my phone in my hand.

Not surprisingly, I struggled to sleep. There were plenty of noises here in this cabin to keep my mind occupied. But unlike the noise machine at home that would play crickets or weather, these noises were real. The authenticity of it all was starting to stress me out. I didn't want to know that I was surrounded by millions of bugs or howling creatures that could try to come in here while I slept. Then I remembered: Ridge was just outside, too. Sleeping in the back of his truck. Protecting me, outside of his housing.

While my hands yearned to scroll my apps, I wrestled with the blanket, tossing and turning. Then, my eyelids started to get heavy as I recalled the feeling of his arms around me. He was a beast of a man; like he could fight off a grizzly with his bare hands. I started to think of his gorgeous face and wondered about who he was on a personal level. I knew he had a strong faith because he talked about God a lot. I'd never been around a guy like that before.

My mind shifted gears to Graham Jones. He was cute, but he paled in comparison to Ridge. Graham, though we'd never met, didn't seem like the type who would sleep outside so I could have the bed. My mind assumed the contrast between them in real life was quite stark.

CHAPTER 16
THE RANGER WAY OF DOING THINGS
EMBER

I awoke to a cold room. The fire was out, and the brightness from the sun rising was slowly filling the windows. I sat up, feeling like I'd just gotten the best sleep of my life. First things first; I checked my phone to see if it magically dried up overnight and was powering on again. But the screen was still black. I squeezed all of the buttons at once, held them individually, and tried to do it with a rhythm in hopes of powering it on, but nothing. For now, I kept it close, just in case a miracle happened and it decided to work. Tiptoeing out of the bed, I peered out the window to see that Ridge's truck was gone. How I slept through that big truck engine powering up and driving away was news to me. I was a pretty light sleeper, and I didn't even have my noise machine on. I tried to refresh myself as best as I could, filling my mouth with toothpaste and water and swirling it around. I was mid-gargle when a knock at the door sent me into a fright, and I nearly swallowed the whole thing. Looking out the door, I saw it was Ridge.

"Good morning," he said, all smiles in his uniform and cowboy hat, handing me a paper bag. Behind him was his pickup truck, back in the same spot as before.

"You snuck up on me," I said, taking the mysterious bag and looking through its contents.

"I thought you might want a change of clothes. I can't promise you will like them, but I can promise they will feel better than what you have on." Inside of the bag was a t-shirt, sweatpants, and a crew neck sweater, all of which was printed with *Yellowstone National Park* in a vibrant, park ranger green. At the bottom of the bag was a pair of men's socks. "I couldn't find anything for women's socks, but I can promise you they have never been worn." He winked, and my entire body turned a shade of pink.

"Thank you so much." I was grateful.

"I have to get to work. Would you want to come with me? I can swing back in a little bit, to let you get ready." My body was still blushing from his wink, and my response came out a little more eager than I intended.

"Yes, just give me a minute." I shut the door on his face and tore into the bathroom. Now that I was in here holding a bag of clothes, the room got even smaller. Everything Ridge grabbed me was in a size extra small. I didn't know if I should be flattered by his realization of my size. Sure, he could have sized up, but then I would have been annoyed that I was wearing baggy clothes. As I slipped into the fresh clothes, they still had room and weren't skintight. I was out of my comfort zone, as I normally wore things very fitted. But under these circumstances, I supposed I didn't mind as much.

"I'm ready," I hollered to Ridge as I ran around to the passenger side of his door before he could open it for me, except he was already there, waiting to be chivalrous.

"I'm just going to grab something inside," he said, as I climbed into the truck. A few minutes later, he returned with a cloth bag full of items.

"What's all that?" I asked.

"The pour over I was telling you about. Plus, some French Roast coffee." He winked again, and my heart rate started matching the speed of the engine as he turned it on.

"Don't you need a change of clothes?" I looked over at him in his uniform.

"This is fresh. I keep an extra set in my truck, in case I sleep out under the stars somewhere and in the pre-dawn light, bathing in the closest non-boiling water." He let out a deep laugh. "I like to do that as much as I can." The thought of being out in the elements, exposed to critters and animals scared me, and I said so.

"I don't think I could do that," I mumbled.

"I didn't ask you to," he said, softly. There was a sweetness to his voice. As my mind started to wander off, we arrived back at the scene of the crime. "I made a call to a wrecker. They think they can be here by noon." Seeing the damage with fresh eyes was shocking. There was truly nothing salvageable to this vehicle, Ridge was right. It was a pancake, and a new feeling took over me. I couldn't quite place what it was. A little bit of embarrassment. A lot of regret. *Shame*, I realized. This was all my fault. It wasn't the tree. It wasn't the weather. I put myself in this situation, without thinking anything through, and this was the consequence. It took everything I had to keep the tears away.

"Should I ride out with the wrecker, then? Or, catch a taxi to the airport?" My question to Ridge seemed to catch him off guard.

"We will figure that out. There's a small regional airport in Cody, west of here. Where are you headin' to?"

"I'm from Denver," I said, feeling sillier by the second. "And this is my first time in Yellowstone."

"Typical tourist," a voice from behind us snickered. We both turned to see it was Travis.

"Excuse me?" I hurled the words at him. Travis just kept walking by.

"Travis, do we have a problem here?" Ridge's words commanded him to stop in his tracks.

"Nah, man. No problem. But I didn't know we were running a bed and breakfast now." His words were filled with sarcasm as he now turned to us and looked me up and down. Ridge didn't say anything back, but crossed his huge, muscular arms. This act alone was enough for Travis to back down and walk away.

"I'm sorry about him," Ridge said to me.

"He's a real jerk, isn't he?" Ridge nodded in reply.

"Extremely unhappy people want to tear down those with hope. On my first day on the job here, he told me he was a pessimistic atheist. That doesn't leave much room for joy, now does it?" I shook my head. "My relationship with the Lord brings me all of the joy I can handle. I can't imagine missing out on that love that we share with our Savior." Listening to Ridge talk about God so freely was a first for me. Sure, I believed in God, and Traci went to church every week without fail. But I'd never been around anyone like him before. And, admittedly, I didn't really understand what Ridge meant when he talked about his relationship with God.

"I believe in God; I do. But when you say, 'relationship', like, does He talk to you or something?" The words sounded so foreign and foolish coming out of my mouth, that I was waiting for Ridge to laugh and correct me. But instead, he agreed.

"Yes. All the time. Especially in nature." He lifted his arms up like he was about to dance in *The Sound of Music*. "He talks to all of us. It's just a matter of if we can hear Him." There was something about this moment in time that struck me as a core memory. Here I was, standing in the middle of the Yellowstone wilderness in Wyoming, looking at a hundred-year-old pine tree that laid on top of my now flattened car, while a gorgeous man was telling me that God talks to me, too, if only I could listen.

At that moment, I felt another uncomfortable feeling. Normally, these bits of unease were fleeting and went unresolved. But the last few days, they were stacking up left and right. Was I feeling... convictions? That hefty word with an even heavier meaning that Traci had thrown around a few times regarding how she chose to live her life. But what conviction was I feeling?

"How about that coffee?" Ridge broke my chain of thoughts, and I welcomed it. Those few minutes of deep consideration of my life were the heaviest mental lifting I had done... ever. I was not very introspective in my life. Nor was I thoughtful for others. I was also a terrible listener. A terrible friend. My heart felt wrecked as I only now remembered that Traci's grandmother was not doing well. I had a phone with me all day yesterday, and I never even thought to call her back.

Ridge opened the door for me once again, and I climbed back in his truck.

"I'm a terrible person," I said out loud, putting my head in my hands, as Ridge was walking around to the driver's side. It felt like a relief to admit it to myself, if anything.

"We all are," Ridge said as he climbed in the driver's side.

"What? I didn't mean for you to hear me," I said, keeping my head in my hands and shaking it back and forth in protest.

"I'm sorry. I have ears like a blind bat. I can hear things for miles." He shrugged, unfazed. "But I mean it. We were all born into sin. We live in a sinful world. None of us are inherently good. Only one man who ever walked the earth was, and that was Jesus." This was all very familiar to me, but at the same time, it was like I was hearing it for the first time. At the station, Ridge put his truck in park.

"So, there's no hope for any of us, then?" I truly didn't know the answer.

"We have hope in Jesus. He died for our sins. If we repent and turn our hearts towards Him, we are washed anew in His grace." This is not the gospel that I'd heard in church growing up.

"What about doing good deeds and going to church and, you know, all of that hard stuff?" I asked, tears forming in my eyes, and for once, I didn't care.

"Well, the Bible does say that faith produces good deeds. But church doesn't make anyone a Christian, though worshiping with other believers is very good for the soul." And there it was, simplified, so even someone like me could understand it.

"So, I just need to repent and believe?" I wiped my eyes, feeling as though an enormous weight had been lifted off of my shoulders.

"Repent. Jesus said to 'take up your cross and follow' Him. We are to turn away from our sinful lives. Have no other idols before God. No more lying, adulterous, deceitful, slanderous ways that get so many."

"I've never committed adultery." I shook my head, not understanding his point.

"Jesus said, just looking with lust is committing adultery in your heart. Just thinking of a sin is committing it. Like I said, the only man to ever be on earth who was sinless was Jesus."

Ridge opened his door, but he lingered for a moment in the conversation. I wasn't ready for it to end. I'd never heard the gospel so simply before this moment, and as the words hit my ears, I was starting to feel the uncomfortable truths of my life. But the moment he did slip out of the truck, I brushed my hand over my dead phone that was in the pocket of the sweatpants, wishing it could work. Needing to forget. Dying for distraction.

Ridge opened my door, and we walked into the station. "Ridge," Travis barked, his hand holding the receiver of a wall phone. "The wolf is almost back." Travis nodded and agreed with someone on the line and hung up, while Ridge walked over to the computer and sat down, analyzing things on the screen.

"Yes, she is." He lets out a low whistle. I sat down by the fireplace and added an extra log. Every time I looked over at the men, Travis' eyes were on me like a hawk after its prey.

"Can I help you?" I finally said to him, as he was making me very uncomfortable with his gaze. And for once, I couldn't even justify it that my outfit was just that special, as I was wearing sweatpants.

Ridge looked up from his focus and back at me. "Let me walk you out," he said to Travis, who rolled his eyes but went for the door. As they left, Ridge left the door partially open. I could hear them speaking clear as day.

"Are we a daycare center now? I'm not sure what Bob would have to say about this."

"She needed help." Ridge stared back at him. "And I'm sure Bob still has some of his humanity left that he would do the same." Travis shook his head.

"Bob has never rescued a damsel in distress." Travis turned away from Ridge, his body language telling me he wasn't ready to go toe to toe with Ridge after all.

"Maybe he never saw one trying to camp in a party store tent." Ridge put his hand on his waist, right above his satellite phone. "Want me to call him right now and ask?" Travis contemplated the scenario for a moment and shook his head.

"No. I don't care what you do." At this, Ridge smiled and laughed.

"You could have fooled me."

CHAPTER 17
SOME PEOPLE DON'T KNOW THEY'RE LOST
RIDGE

Sharing words with Travis was like poking a bear with a fish. Sometimes it's receptive, because it likes fish. Another time, it might ignore you. Then, it's angry and out for blood.

Travis had a natural anger to him that was extremely concerning. If he didn't push people away so much, he might have found that the world wasn't what he thought it was, but at the same time, he was his own person. He made his own choices. Something about me ruffled his feathers, but those feathers were already sparse and falling out like a neglected parrot. Travis just couldn't see this for himself.

We finally dispersed after arguing about my helping Ember, when the phone inside the station rang. He left, headed where, I didn't care. We both needed some time apart from one another. I prayed that when he returned, he'd have an attitude adjustment.

Inside the ranger station, Ember was facing the fire, wearing the sweatpants I bought for her in the gift shop this morning. The large shop that didn't even open to the general public for another week, but the manager owed me a favor for not fining him for trying to take a selfie with a buffalo my first day on the job, letting him off with a warning instead. Not that I would have fined him—I just wanted him to know better. I was more of a common sense approach to life and let things shake out as they should. Stupid games win stupid prizes, as my dad always said. Still, I'm glad that I decided to chat with him instead. It sure came in handy when I needed to buy a few things ahead of the store opening.

I knew the outfit was something she wasn't used to wearing, and I was trying my hardest not to check her out any more than what was appropriate, but she looked great in the sweatpants. I never thought I'd think that about anyone.

"Sorry about him," I said in passing, before I answered the phone. It was embarrassing to be associated with Travis sometimes.

"This is Taylor with Yellowstone Wrecker," the scratchy voice on the other end of the line said.

"Hi, Taylor. Are we still expecting you this afternoon?" The fact that they were calling me right now meant, probably not.

"That's why I'm calling. There's been a landslide outside of the East Gate of Yellowstone and we're waiting on loaders to come clear it. I would just drive around but that would be eight hours I just don't have, and I am off the next two days, and I can't budge on that because I'm heading to visit my folks. I'm sorry, but it will be a few days before I can make it, and I understand if you need to call someone else."

"Call me before you leave, and I'll let you know if anything's changed." We hung up the call.

The feelings that followed were... complicated. Was I a little disappointed that the flattened car wouldn't be pulled out from under that tree? Yes. Was I also overjoyed that this meant I got to spend more time with this beautiful, yet also *complicated* woman? Also, yes.

"It looks like that tow truck won't be here for a few days," I said, treading carefully and speaking slowly as if the news might shatter her already fragile feelings. While I didn't completely understand this woman, I did understand her upset at the situation. While I waited for her to say something, I clicked on an email that came in just moments before. "But we can call another company. They have them throughout Montana as well. Depends what your budget is because this guy is the closest."

"Hmm," was her initial response. "I mean, the more affordable, the better. This is going to be a costly event."

"You're welcome to stay in my place while we wait." To this, she stood up.

"Why? Why are you doing this? I don't... understand!" She turned to me, and I was met with anger.

"Why? Because you need a place to stay. Nothing is open here yet. I can't just leave you to weather the elements outside."

"But you are! For me. Why?" She stomped her foot as she waited for an answer. An answer I didn't know how to articulate.

"Because you... are a damsel in distress." I couldn't help but laugh as I said the words, repeating what Travis had accused me of and knowing it was true. "We are called to help the helpless." I put my hands in the air in defeat. I didn't know what this woman wanted from me, so I just gave up the conversation while she looked at me with a mad expression on her face.

"That is so... manly of you." Her tone was flat. "Thank you." The words slipped out of her lips like a secret.

"You're welcome. Now, I have to go inspect a report that came in of grizzlies nearing some winter kill. Do you want to tag along?"

*****

Having a beautiful woman riding shotgun in my ranger truck was a blast. Total upgrade from curmudgeon Travis. But it wasn't just about looks with Ember... There was definitely something about her that drew me in.

Maybe it was the fact that she was so difficult. *Lord, do I even know what's happening here?* I asked God for guidance on the matter as we left Fishing Bridge and headed towards West Thumb. Ember immediately reached for the radio as we pulled out onto the road, and I didn't object. I wanted to know what made this woman tick.

Seconds later, the speakers were blaring a country crooner. "Do you mind if we turn it down a little? I need to be able to hear this." I pointed to the radio attached to my dashboard. She nodded and took the volume down a few decibels, but I still couldn't hear myself think, so every few minutes I casually turned the dial down while I struck up a conversation. At this rate, in ten minutes, it would be off.

"So, how did you sleep last night?" I asked, hitting that radio dial.

"At first, not good. I kept hearing howling. You're not a werewolf, are you?" She laughed and scrunched her nose.

"No, but how cool would that be? To live among a pack of wolves for a day every month." I smiled, and she just shrugged.

"Then, I slept great, actually. Something about the inability to check my phone made me sleep through the night. Who knew?" I nodded, knowing the phone thing was really bothering her, and I hoped that we could distract her from that today as she rode along with me to this scene.

"I'm sorry about your phone," I said, meaning it.

"It's just what I use for *everything*. I feel crippled without it. I mean, what do you do without a phone? I can't imagine."

"I'm just out here, living." I shrugged, realizing that made it sound like I was being snarky. "I've never had a need for a smart phone. Where I come from, you check the weather by looking out the window. If the windsock is indicating wind, you look out to the West, where we have one that is made from an old towing chain. If *that* is indicating wind, you know you're about to get blown off your feet." Her eyes widened, and I noticed she seemed very distracted by her dead phone still. It was clear there were more factors at play here. While no one is perfect, I could tell this was something she needed to pray for.

Pulling into the West Thumb area, I spotted Travis' vehicle in a pull off. I let out a sigh; I was not ready to see this guy, and I was hoping that God would intervene somehow. Travis just wasn't a kind person nor did he make it pleasant to be around him. If only Bob could have reassigned Travis to somewhere else?

The report that came through this morning was that a sow grizzly bear and her two cubs were about two hundred yards from a bison carcass that had perished over the winter and had been preserved under the snow melt. The bears wouldn't pass up the opportunity at it, as they were just coming out of hibernation and this was too easy. After parking the truck, I grabbed my binoculars and opened the door, standing on the running boards to see where the carcass was. I spotted it almost instantly, and now, I would wait for the bears to show.

I looked back over my shoulder at Travis' vehicle. He preferred to drive a compact car around the park, while I insisted on traversing in this F-350 truck. Using my binoculars, I expected to see Travis drinking out of his coffee thermos or taking notes on some fauna with a laptop. But instead, his vehicle was empty. A bad feeling took over me as I looked back to the expectant grizzly area and searched harder.

CHAPTER 18
I DON'T DO DRAMA, BUT THIS IS IMPORTANT
RIDGE

At the edge of the geyser basin, where the geothermal activity was too dangerous for people, I saw Travis. "What in the world?" I said aloud. I jumped back in the truck, turning on the ignition. The loud music immediately blasting, I tapped the dial, turning it off completely. "I'm sorry, but this isn't really the time or the place," I mumbled to Ember under my breath.

"Is everything okay?" she asked, and I shook my head.

"There is a group of grizzlies headed right for where Travis is standing right now, by a dangerous geyser basin that is known to erupt randomly. Either this guy has a death wish or he's just that clueless," I said, regretting my words instantly. I parked the truck only a hundred yards closer, but in a life-or-death situation, it might make all the difference in the world. Jumping back out, I grabbed two cans of bear spray from the back door and put one in each hand.

"When will you be back?" she asked with her eyes as wide as they would go.

"Hopefully, soon. If I don't come back, just lock the doors and hit this button right here." I pointed to my emergency beacon on the radio. "I have one on me, too." My SPOT device was always on me and ready.

There was no time for anything else. I left Ember in the truck and headed on foot to tell Travis he was in immediate danger, praying for my safety the whole time.

The Lord is my shepherd. This verse had always calmed me in times of anguish. When I was little, I used to go out every day after school with my BB gun and husky. We would roam around the mountains and the valleys until it was dinner time; with my dad working the cattle all day until sundown, we'd usually pull up around the same time, ready to eat. But one day, a storm swept through the area, and I hunkered down under some trees. My husky, Tommy, nudged me to get back up when the rainstorm had moved west, but once I climbed out from under the trees, I had gotten turned around. We ended up wandering for hours in that forested area and the fear started to spread in my bones. *Even though I walk through the darkest valley, I will fear no evil, for You are with me; Your rod and Your staff, they comfort me.*

It was these verses that calmed me in this trial and helped me keep my wits about me. When the sun started to set, and I was still off course, I gathered some small branches and made a fire. It was the smoke from the pine boughs that led my dad right to me, where he came to my rescue just an hour later.

Sometimes, we send smoke signals to God, and we don't even know it. Ember was doing it now. The woman was clearly addicted to her phone and social media. She had to have that distraction from herself. The loud music, the fire. I wondered what would happen if for once, she encountered herself on the trail? Or, God? Would she relish and cling to Him or would she still reach for her phone?

As I got closer to Travis, I was within earshot, but I did not want to surprise any bears and get mauled in the process. So, I eased into the noise by humming. Yet, the only song I could think of to hum was *Happy Birthday*. Travis turned and gave me a strange look.

"What are you doing here?" he asked with suspicion.

"I could ask you the same question." Looking over my shoulder at the bison carcass, I knew at any moment the trees would reveal a pack of hungry grizzly bears.

"I'm monitoring the geothermal activity at this geyser basin."

"You're about to be a target for hungry apex predators. We've got a sow and two large cubs on the move to have at that." I pointed to the carcass. "I drive out here to monitor the situation and then I see you. You know better than this, Travis." I turned, satisfied after warning him about the impending danger and expecting him to follow me back to our vehicles. Instead, he stayed put.

"I'm just doing my job," he said. I turned back to him and watched him write down some notes about the bubbling geyser.

"Next to a carcass? In spring, while standing in an active grizzly territory? What is up with you, man? You got a death wish?" Travis just shrugged. I realized then that he did. "Look, Travis. I know we got off on the wrong foot. I know you don't like me much, but there is so much more to life than this, buddy. You can find happiness. You could get a job somewhere warm." Every few seconds I looked over my shoulder, expecting to see a grizzly tearing through the trees with me in its crosshairs while I stood here pleading with Travis.

"I don't hate you, Ridge. I just don't understand why you're so happy all the time. And don't even get me started on the woman." Travis rolled his eyes as he held a little clipboard. For all I knew, he was drawing doodles and stick figures on that thing while I had my back to impending danger, with two aerosol cans at my defense.

"It's because of Jesus," I said. "The hope I have. The joy He gives. He wants to give it to you too, Travis. All you have to do is accept."

We stood out there for a few more minutes in silence while Travis looked away. My ears were alert to every noise originating from the forested area, and finally, the noise of a tree branch snapping echoed through the area. There weren't that many animals that were heavy enough to break a limb of a tree when stepping on it. Finally, Travis relented.

"Okay. Thanks. But right now, we better go." Relief washed over me. Not for myself—God had all of my days written in His book, and only He knew how my life would unfold, but for Travis... As we rapidly walked back, we both had our cans of bear spray handy just in case. "Thank you for coming," he whispered under his breath, not able to look me in the eye.

"You don't need to thank me. I was here anyway. You would have done it for me." Travis protested.

"No, I wouldn't. And for that, I'm sorry. I really do want to think about this change of heart. I can't keep this going. The negativity is so deep in my life that I'm exhausted. Honestly, I was ready to be taken out by bears just to end it. But then I said a little prayer. I've never done it before, so I don't know if I did it right. I just said, 'God, are You really there?' And not two seconds later, You show up, in all of your cheerful, annoying glory, and it becomes clear to me."

"I'm happy I could come and annoy you in your time of need," I teased. Travis, who would normally sneer or snicker at any possible joke, laughed.

"Nah, man. I mean it in a good way. You're just good, and that's why you bother me so much. Because I'm not." I stopped in my tracks, looking back. The bears had found the carcass. The huge animals looked like the size of a Buick. We were far enough away that, unless we started grilling some ribs over an open fire, I didn't think they were going to leave that for us.

"I'm not good, Travis. Here's the thing: We are all sinners, born into it. We all fall short of the glory of God. Nothing we say or do in this life will earn us salvation if we don't repent for our sins and accept the free gift of salvation. In this, we are born again."

"What if I don't even know what my sins are?" I prayed to God for the right answer as I considered his question.

"I have an extra Bible I will give you back at the ranger station. In there, you will find the Ten Commandments and the guidance that Jesus himself gave. But for now, just lead with love in all things that you do."

"That's like the opposite of what I've been doing,"

When we reached my truck, Travis reached out and shook my hand, looking me in the eye for the first time that I could recall in the short amount of time that I'd known him. "Thank you," he said, before taking the long walk back to his car.

"What was that?" Ember asked, as I opened the door. Seeing her was like taking a breath of air after swimming underwater.

"Travis just needed a change of heart," I said, not feeling like I needed to expand on it. Ember looked straight ahead. "Were you okay in here? I'm sorry I was gone for so long."

I was guessing it had been about twenty minutes, and I was sure she was bored to tears. I could have left her at the station where at least there was a computer.

"No, that's okay. I was bored, but maybe I need to be bored." Before I could consider her words, I saw more movement at the bison. Using the binoculars, I realized a fourth bear joined in. "Can I take a look?" Ember asked.

"Are you sure? It's a little gory." I held the binoculars out to her, letting it be her decision.

"Yes. It doesn't bother me. I know there's a circle to life out here," she said confidently, as she peered into the lenses before putting them down quickly. "And I wasn't prepared for *that,*" she laughed, as a matter-of-factly. "Wow. Let me just take a breather for a second. Okay, I'm going to try again." When she looked the second time, I watched her. All sorts of expressions came onto her mouth, and I found myself wondering what it would be like to kiss her. I shook the thought from my mind. *God, I want to reserve these feelings for my future wife. Please shield my heart if Ember is not that woman.* It was a bold prayer, but I had bold faith and very much needed God's hand in my life.

"Well? What do you think?" I asked her, as she set the binoculars down on the median in between our seats.

"I thought I'd seen it all," she said, shaking her head. "I mean, I've watched *millions* of videos online. I've pretty much scrolled through the internet every day, all day, for years. But, I've never seen anything like that." She paused. "It wasn't brutal, though. It was a mother bear leading her offspring to food. The animal was already deceased. By natural causes?" she asked, turning to me.

"Yes. The winter here is harsh. This area alone can see thirty feet of snow, easily. But it's also majestic, and some of the creatures thrive. Just look at the Trumpeter Swan; it could be minus twenty degrees out, but the thermal temps from the geysers make it so things don't always freeze over out here. It's remarkable to see one float down a river in January, I'll tell ya that." I reminisced of the winter tours I'd taken through here on a snowmobile.

"That's amazing. I assumed that any and all waterfowl flew south for the winter. I know I would."

"They can, but as long as they have food, some choose to stay."

"Let me guess. You would be the duck that would stay?" She turned to me and scrunched her nose again.

"Yes, you got me. I don't think I could live anywhere else outside of the Rockies." And for a fleeting second in time, we shared a moment, as we looked into each other's eyes. She broke the gaze, reaching for the radio dial before hesitating.

"Oh, is it okay if we turn this back on?"

"Sure. I'm going to close this area down. Then we can wrangle up some lunch. How does that sound?" Her smile rivaled the light of the sun, and I got back out of the truck, retrieving my fences and signs from the bed.

CHAPTER 19
WHEN THE WILD WINS
EMBER

Sitting here in this rugged truck with no phone to scroll was brutal. And with Ridge away, I didn't feel comfortable starting the engine so I could have used the radio, but at least then I would've had something to sing to. Something to pass the time. So instead, I watched him walk as if I was counting his steps. I noticed the rhythm to his muscles as he went quickly to the man standing at the geyser. *A man on a mission*, I thought. But a mission for what?

It almost looked like an altercation happening when he reached him. The two men talked and talked, Ridge keeping one eye on the bison at all times with the frequency that he kept looking at it. My eyes focused on his every movement, to keep my mind far away from our earlier conversation. After a long time, the men were out of sight. They must have been on the walk back. Out of habit, I checked my phone again. Still broken.

I leaned back in the seat. With nothing else to do, I finally thought back to those feelings I had this morning. Convictions. I felt nudged to see them—to feel them. But I didn't even know what to do. Suddenly, it became clear to me as I came to terms with the fact that I was addicted to my phone. I was reliant on social media. But technology was the god that I worshipped, and I couldn't be any farther from Christ if I had tried. My ways were all self-serving. My mind was set on earthly goals and not heavenly treasures. And I felt extremely overwhelmed by these revelations.

The fact that they took me by surprise was almost as shocking; Traci had been hinting at these things for years. But I never listened to her, because I wasn't a good friend. I wasn't good at anything. Like Ridge said, none of us are. And yet, Ridge was a wonderfully generous man who would have given up his own cabin for a stranger like me. Would I have done the same? No.

"God?" I asked aloud, waiting for the sky to open up and strike me down with a rod of lightning. Heck, I was almost struck by lightning just yesterday. Perhaps God had been trying to tell me something with this experience all along. "Are you there?" I closed my eyes and waited. My mind was riddled with the sins

I'd committed. The guilt of them. The shame of my life. Where did I go from here? "God, please wash me anew. I want to start over," I said, my words trembling as I spoke. Was I ready to start over? The doubt chased my words the moment I said them. I wondered if this was the devil working overtime in my mind, and the realization of that thought—something I would never have considered before— was proof that God was here with me. And so was the enemy.

I opened my eyes up, first seeing my phone. This had caused me a lot of pain, I thought. I wasn't ready to just chuck it out the window or anything. Truthfully, if it had still been in working order, I would've loaded it up so fast my head would have spun. But in this silence, in the technology void that I was sitting in, where only an AM/FM radio could reach a signal and play old crooners who didn't give me the dose of dopamine that my brain was so heavily altered to crave, I felt like something else was happening. God was trying to reach me. *Would I know how to answer the call?*

When Ridge returned to the truck, it appeared that he and Travis were old pals. They even shook hands. Travis' eyes grazed over me for a second, and I expected backlash from sitting here with him as if I was on a park ranger ride along, but nothing came of it. Travis just looked right past me. He seemed different, like he'd had a change of heart, but it was shocking since just earlier this morning, he had been a royal jerk.

When I asked Ridge what that was about, it wasn't lost on me that he smelled like the outdoors. A scent of pine and musk filled the truck, and it was nearly intoxicating to my senses. It took everything I had to ignore the fact that I liked how this guy *smelled,* and he was not even wearing a trendy or popular men's cologne. This guy was naturally scented well, and his pheromones were communicating with mine. To distract myself, I asked to see what he was studying so intently through the binoculars. He hesitated but ultimately agreed.

Watching giant grizzlies feast sent shivers down my spine, and I had to pause for a moment to regroup. When I looked again, something in my brain activated. It was like watching a social media video online, but in live time. It started to scratch that itch, though the topic of this real-life reel wasn't my favorite. I was enthralled by the grizzly bears. They were such powerful creatures that I was disappointed I couldn't share photos of them on my social media. As I watched them, my heart still yearned to see it from the face of my phone instead of my own eyes, but I welcomed the distraction.

When I was done looking, we shared some idle chat about ducks. Ridge was a huge nature lover, and I was starting to see why. It was thrilling to see the bears from the comfort of safety, but knowing he was just mere steps from them a little while ago shook me. Whatever Ridge was doing with Travis, he risked his life to do it.

Then, it happened. I accidentally shared eye contact with him. I didn't mean to do it because I didn't do it with anyone. Truthfully, I didn't know why I had a hard time with it. It probably had something to do with my extreme self-avoidance pattern that I was stuck in. But for that fleeting chance meeting of our eyes, I saw more of Ridge. He was more than just my protector. I thought he was meant for more. I broke the gaze, unable to have him seeing right to my soul the way he did. Every time he looked at me, I started to see myself differently, and I wasn't prepared for all of this change. Sure, I hadn't changed anything yet, but I might have. It was never too late to change.

I reached for the radio dial, my fingers ready to blast the music to drown out my inner monologue, when I hesitated. Something inside of me nudged my heart; *oh, just those convictions again.* Was this good for everyone, or just me? When I asked him about the radio, I could tell he was just being gracious to me. Which he'd been nothing but. He agreed, telling me he had to fence off the area so some random tourist didn't accidentally wander in. My fingers were still waiting on the dial as I watched him get out of the truck. He retrieved signs from his truck bed and started setting them up around the parking area. I watched him move. His muscles were protruding through his uniform. He had legs like a racehorse and arms like Thor. It wasn't until he came back that I realized that the radio was still off.

Listening as he alerted people on his radio about the area, two other voices agreed to come monitor the situation. We waited for a moment, one of them appearing within seconds. Ridge waved, as the man's smile turned to confusion when he saw me in Ridge's passenger seat.

"I'm not going to get you in trouble, am I?" *Wow, this is new for me*, I thought immediately. Since when did I care about consequences for others?

"Doubt it. I'm not breaking any rules. In fact, I'm following them by protecting visitors." Ridge peeked over at me out of the corner of his eye. It was all it took for me to blush. We drove back to his small cabin where he excused himself. "I'll be right back."

Ridge returned ten minutes later with a large bag, and we drove in silence to a nearby picnic area. After watching him at the bear site, suddenly I was very aware of him and his attractiveness. Now, that didn't mean I liked him. Many people were attractive, but there had to be mutual interests and compatibility. Like Graham and me. We both loved social media, and he liked all of my photos, so I knew we both liked my online persona. Just thinking the thought made me feel lame at first, but I reminded myself that I was a city girl. I didn't do these sorts of things just for fun; this was for a brand deal. One that, with my phone broken, would probably be my last.

"Are you warm enough?" Ridge asked, as we pulled into a parking area and he grabbed the bag out of the back seat with his right arm. I was plenty warm; in fact, almost overheating as he'd had the heat cranked up for me this whole time. I nodded, pulling the lever on my door handle and when I looked back to him, he was gone. My door opened the rest of the way, and I laughed as he helped me out.

"Such a gentleman. Thank you." He tipped his cowboy hat in reply. "Did you ever find your ranger hat?" He shook his head.

"No. That thing is a goner. I'm not too sad about it, though. I prefer a Stetson."

"It looks good on you," I said, the words out of my mouth before I could contain them. My cheeks flushed; I put on my best avoidance and act like I had never said it and hoped that it went away.

"Thank you, darlin'," he said, with enough masculinity to overthrow a nation. I closed my eyes, feeling like I might have lost consciousness because suddenly, I was not just acknowledging his attraction. Instead, I was a magnet to his force field. I was the moon to his sun, and my feelings were officially in orbit. The only question was, what did this mean?

CHAPTER 20
FOLLOWING THE WRONG SIGNAL
EMBER

We walked through a small, wooded area to a picnic table that sat on a riverbank. There was a chill in the air but admittedly, it felt good. Maybe I was becoming outdoorsy? With no chair to pull out for me, Ridge waited until I was seated before he seated himself. While I had been put off by his chivalry at first, even a little annoyed by it, I had to say: I could get used to this treatment. He was raised to treat a woman like a queen. I shook the thought from my head, physically putting my face in my hands and rubbing my eyes.

"You okay?" he asked, pulling out a lunch spread that looked like he had the picnic table catered.

"I'm great," I said, a tone of sarcasm lightly woven in. Meanwhile, I was struggling with myself, my evolving attraction to a stranger, and my brand new convictions. I didn't know which would win this fight, but for the first time in my life, I let go of the control that I'd been fooling myself that I'd had all this time. Something in the back of my mind nudged me, letting me know that only God had that.

Ridge made sandwiches with crusty, artisan bread. I devoured mine.

"This is so good," I said in between bites. No more picking at my food or just eating salads out here. Not only did all of this outdoor stuff make me hungrier, but I was also craving foods with more sustenance.

"Glad you like it. My family makes bread as a hobby. I brought a few loaves with me when I got here last week." If my mouth hadn't been full of food, my jaw would have dropped.

"You've only been here for a week?" I finally stammered in between bites, realizing I wasn't even making an attempt to eat lady-like, and I was so hungry and the food so good, I didn't even care. Ridge nodded, pulling out crackers, cheese, and water from the bag and a small pouch of granola, *my favorite.* "How is that even possible? I feel like you know everything about this place."

"I don't know about that, but I grew up coming here. I'm from up north of here in Montana. I think I told you; we have a big ranch up there and were fortunate enough to spend time in Yellowstone often. I think some of it is second nature to me and knowing what to do in certain situations. Like the bears. I know I can't have tourists wandering in there looking to take a selfie." He winked and if it wasn't so true, I would have laughed. Mostly, I was reading into his wink like it was a top-secret message from the Pentagon. Things started to shift in my mind; is this how he treated all the ladies or did he like me? Did I want him to like me? Could he like someone like me even? We were polar opposites in every sense of the word. Then, it dawned on me: He could already be taken, and this would let me know right away if he was just this kind of guy.

"Do you have a girlfriend?" I blurted out, not even considering there could be a better way of asking the question. He looked surprised by my question as he chewed some of his food. Ridge was a handsome eater; I added that to his scorecard, too. Didn't take bites that were too big. He wasn't messy about it. No mustard on the front of his shirt.

"No," he said in a way that made me think there was a follow up or snarky comment coming, but it was just followed by silence.

"Okay, then." The wheels in my mind went on overdrive.

"And you? Do you have a boyfriend?" I thought of Graham Jones. Someone I'd been casually flirting with online, but nothing had come of it. We hadn't even met yet, and I wasn't sure if we even would.

"No. Not really," I said, instantly regretting it. Ridge nodded. I made it sound like I was a serial dater or seeing multiple men, when in reality I'd never even had a boyfriend past high school! So, the back pedaling began. "I mean, I've been chatting with someone online a little. But we haven't even met, and I don't know if I even want to meet him." There. Crisis averted. I went from a girl seeing fifteen different guys on a rotation of dates in an effort to never pay for a meal again to a quiet, pensive homebody who strung people along in fear of making a decision. *Much better.*

"I see. Well, tell me about this guy. What does he do?" Not Ridge sizing him up? I wondered. If only there was more to say about Graham than I knew.

"He's like me. A social media influencer." Just the words coming out of my mouth sounded preposterous. I wished I could have heard what Ridge really thought about that.

"What does that even mean, 'influencer'?" Ridge laughed and I knew, instinctively, that he knew Graham was not a threat to him. Just like I knew Graham and Ridge did not even compare in the slightest.

"Like the brand deal thing; brands will send gifts and pay for collaborations to get their goods in front of the masses on social media for exposure. It's a currency on its own," I said, nodding. This was the only thing I knew for certain. Everything else in my life was up in the air.

"And this guy—he does the same thing? With what kind of brands? Like protein or supplements?" I held back my laughter at the thought of Graham with protein. He certainly wasn't a body builder like Ridge looked like he could be, naturally.

"More like, bike related things." I didn't want to say someone sent him a retro banana-seat bicycle or those spandex pants with the padding on the rear.

"Oh, so he's into motorcycles? We have an old Harley at the ranch that I like to take out once a summer, but it's got a great muffler on it. Not one of those that disrupt every ear within a hundred miles." I took another bite, chewing slowly so that I could hold off leveling with him for a moment. There was no shame in bicycles, but in comparison to what Ridge thought, it was just different. And there was something about Ridge that made me embarrassed to talk about Graham. I was regretting bringing it up at all.

"Bicycles. Think, Tour de France." Ridge was very gracious about this, just nodding to himself. No laughter or smiles, and now I was starting to wonder why I thought he would be a jerk about it. He was not a jerk. I was the only jerk here.

"So, why aren't you sure if you want to meet him, then?" Ridge continued the conversation in a tone of... hope; he gave me hope. Did I want hope?

"Well, I don't know. He hasn't really asked to meet yet, and there's another gal that he's liking all of her photos, too. She's in Africa right now. Hard to compete with that," I said in defeat.

"You shouldn't have to compete with anyone, Ember. And you would never feel that way a day in your life if you chose the right man." We did it again—the eye contact was hard to avoid, but this time, I stayed put. There was nowhere to run to, no radio to turn on. No fire alarm to pull. His searching eyes looked into mine, and I let him. I put my sandwich down, never before having had this feeling. But what was it? I stood slowly, leaning over the table, and electricity ran through my body as he did the same. At this second, I felt like if I didn't kiss him, I would die. He leaned in, his body language telling me he felt the same way. Right before our lips could touch, there was a hesitancy to him. As he stood still, we shared a moment so personal, so intimate, that I nearly fell backwards.

No parts of our bodies touched but I held his gaze, and there we stood, frozen in time. The creek and tall trees were the only witness to our exchange. When he surprisingly pulled away, my eyes were locked in on him, searching for meaning in the moment. Thinking that maybe, he would walk around the table and kiss me. Maybe he would sit us side by side instead. The adrenaline shot through all of the veins in my body as I waited for what was next. I waited anxiously for him to take the lead, as he has done in every other moment since we met. But instead, after pulling away, he sat back down and looked at the creek.

"I'm sorry, Ember. That wasn't right, and I want you to know that my intentions were just to help you, and though I think you are the most beautiful woman ever, this wasn't part of my plan."

"You think I'm beautiful?" I asked, choosing to not hear the rest of it. I know Ridge wasn't that type of sleazy guy with a one track mind, and that near kiss was very much my own agenda. What I was interested in hearing more about were his thoughts about me.

"Of course I do. You know you're gorgeous," he smiled, but looked strained. Borderline upset. Again, I ignored it.

"I think you are totally hot, too." I smiled, hoping this would pull him out of his funk. It didn't.

"We better go. I need to check in with my boss," Ridge said while getting up. Fear replaced excitement; was the near-kiss bad for Ridge in some way? I felt internal fireworks, and we didn't even touch. Did he feel the opposite? The attraction I felt for this man went from acknowledgement to a fire within my soul in the course of a fifteen- minute lunchbreak. As ridiculous as it sounded and felt, I'd never felt this way towards anyone. I'd strategically avoided anything real my entire life to avoid getting hurt. That realization alone hit me like a brick.

*****

We rode back to his station in silence. I kept looking at him, but he was staring straight ahead, focused on the winding roads. His facial expression said it all: he was fighting something inside of him, just like he said—that our near-kiss wasn't right. Now that the moment had passed, I was grasping at my thoughts to know just what wasn't right about it. It had felt right. It was the most right thing I'd ever encountered, in fact. I worked up the courage to ask him, but my words fell short.

"May I ask you a question?" I whispered, as we were about to pull into the ranger station. He was turning the wheel like he was the captain of a naval ship.

"Yes," he said, stoicism bleeding from his voice.

"Why did you say that, um, that wasn't right?" I couldn't say the word kiss, because we didn't. Besides, it had been so much more than that. He let out a sigh, putting the truck into park.

"Because I am waiting for marriage to share physical intimacy with a woman. I live intentionally, and that includes now. I didn't mean to let that get so close, of course. But I wanted to. I've wanted to kiss you since the moment I saw you. Truthfully, this has progressed a little differently and faster than I ever anticipated, and I let my guard down. That was not my intention, and I want to make that clear. And now I don't know what to do, but I know it needs to start with prayer." Hearing his convictions made me do something out of the ordinary. As he got out of the truck, I requested some time in here to think.

"If it's alright, can I just sit in here for a few minutes? Do some... praying of my own." The words were foreign as they came out of my mouth. I hadn't prayed in... Well, other than the prayer I half spoke yesterday, it had been far too long. Ridge gave me a pained smile and agreed. And for the first time in my adult life, I chose silence to encounter something within—and greater—than myself. "God? I need Your help."

I sat in silence in the truck for what felt like the rest of the day. The truck was turned off, so I didn't have a clock to reference, but it must have been hours. Checking my phone every few minutes to see if miracles could still happen, I used all of my breath to blow into the part where chords plug in so I could accelerate the drying process. I was more deranged each time that it might just light up. The thought process was that perhaps it was still drying out. *Whatever*, I thought. I'm supposed to be praying. So, I closed my eyes and tried again.

"God?" I said aloud, picturing clouds and revealing a golden, glowing sky. "God, I'm here. And like I said, I, uh—I really need your help." I paused, when all of the lyrics to my favorite song came into my head. Then, a really funny meme I saw recently came back into memory. A feeling of yearning to send a few texts and phone calls. I checked my phone again. Nothing. Maybe it had dried out but now the battery was just really dead? Afterall, I didn't charge it last night. Could that be it? I wondered. I'd never not charged it overnight, so I didn't know how long the battery could really last. I couldn't believe I didn't think of this sooner!

CHAPTER 21
FAITH LOOKS DIFFERENT OUT HERE
EMBER

Jumping out of the truck, I ran into the ranger station. "I need a phone cord!" I exclaimed, paying no mind that Ridge was currently busy. The wall phone was up to his ear, and he was examining some sort of radar map on the computer.

"Yeah, that's what I thought, too. Okay. Thanks, Bob. I'll keep you posted." He hung up the phone, and I repeated my statement.

"I need a phone cord, Ridge. Do you have one?" He shook his head.

"Told you. I don't have a cell phone. Sorry," he said, a shaky tone to his voice.

"Okay. Maybe, uh, Travis has one?" I hated to get him involved, as he wasn't very kind to me, but this was kind of an emergency.

"I don't know. I can ask him next time I see him," he shrugged. "But right now, I have to go on site. Raya the wolf is about to make a re-introduction to the park, and I want to see it for myself." I watched as he gathered up a few things from his desk: his walkie talkie, a thermos, and a small tracker. He also pulled open a drawer and pulled out a digital camera. I was floored, ignoring the fact that he had just spoken a woman's name.

"I didn't know you had a digital camera this whole time? You said you had an old fashioned one." I stomped my foot in surprise. Ridge looked confused.

"This belongs to the park. It's not mine." There was a tone of annoyance in his voice that made me wish I could have taken back what I had just said. But it was too late now and besides, he thought I was beautiful, but he didn't want to kiss me. So, it was probably not going anywhere. I needed to decide if I was pursuing this—whatever this even was—or my career as a social media influencer. I was leaning towards the latter.

"I could use it for my brand deal. Take a few photos of this, uh, experience. Download the photos and email them to myself. No one would have to know I used it." My idea was airtight, but Ridge didn't look so sure.

"That's not entirely true," Ridge said, his back to me.

"What do you mean?"

"I will know you used it, which is a violation of what I agreed to." He sighed, turning to me. "This is quite the expensive camera, is all. Breaking it would mean that the park would have to replace it, and... I don't want that on my record right off the bat. Do you understand?" The camera in his hands may have well been a carrot dangling on a stick. I didn't understand.

"I won't break it. I'm a gen-z, after all. I was raised with technology, and I'm careful with things." Pleading with him now, I hated that my voice sounded like I was begging. I stiffened up. "It's for my work. If you don't mind." Hesitating, he finally relented.

"Okay. If you want to stay behind, you can use it this afternoon while I scope things out with Raya. But I'm really going to need it tomorrow, so keep it safe, please."

"Scouts honor," I said, giving him a salute. "By the way," I spun on my heels, having had another loose end to tie up. "Who is Raya?" Was this woman someone who I was unknowingly competing for Ridge with? Was I wanting to woo Ridge at all? Excitement crossed his face.

"She's a wolf that was relocated to New Mexico and after being released there, she's traveled all the way back here in search of something." Hearing the words at first, I didn't get what the big deal was.

"So? Why is this important?"

"Raya is returning to her mate. He must have been left behind."

"That's kind of far-fetched, right? Like to think that an animal could have a bond so strong that it would travel *how* many miles? Maybe she just likes to travel. Has anyone considered that?" Ridge shook his head.

"Raya knows where she belongs in the world." He left without another word. A mix of shame and embarrassment from my talking points spread through my mind. Ridge didn't seem very impressed with my logic, but could a wolf really travel this far because of a bond with another animal? Could it travel for *love?* The coolness of his personality from where it was before lunch was striking. After our near-kiss, I thought he completely changed his mind about how he was going to feel about me. *That's fine*, I thought to myself. But it didn't feel fine. It felt awful, adding to my stranded, phoneless, carless situation.

It was time to get a grip on the situation: I was holding a solution to some of my problems. So, first things first: I turned on the camera. There were a few buttons that weren't clearly labeled, and it instantly took me to the pictures already on the camera. I turned it off and on again, not wanting to mess with any of those photos. Laughing as I imagined myself accidentally deleting a photo of a rare white tiger or something. Were there tigers in Yellowstone? I shuddered at the thought.

My mood had lifted remarkably since I'd been holding a piece of technology in my hands. I started snapping all of the pictures I wished I could before, the aesthetic ranger station being the first thing. Taking one of the cute wood stove and the roaring fire inside. Then, the vintage-looking thermos that sat nearby. A small cord of wood stacked perfectly in a metal basket. I turned the camera to myself, as a selfie of sorts, before I remembered I was clad in a tourist shop sweatsuit and no makeup or false lashes that my followers were used to seeing, and immediately changed my mind.

After a few snaps, my eyes made contact with the wall phone, and I thought that I had better call and check-in with my mom. Setting the camera down, I walked over and dialed the number. We talked for a handful of minutes, and I told her about the bears, the cabin I was staying in, and the wolf that was making her way back into the park. She was genuinely excited to hear that I was having a great adventure, which made me change my attitude a little. *This is an adventure*, I thought to myself, and one that I would never forget. We ended the conversation with her telling me she was proud of me for surviving without social media for a few days, and I cringed hearing the words. I didn't know how much I was actually surviving, considering I'd been using the ranger station computer to stay connected this whole time.

I considered calling Traci when I was done but by the time my mother and I finally hung up the phone, I was staring at Ridge's computer. I decided to go in and check my socials. After all, I might have had some new photos to upload here shortly. The moment I sat down and logged in, a message from Graham Jones popped up in my inbox.

Hey, Ember. I saw you were in Yellowstone National Park. I'm actually headed that direction today and was wondering if you wanted to chill while I'm there?

Graham

I did it. It was happening! My fingers hit the keys faster than my mind could catch up.

Why, yes, I am here. For a few more days, maybe. I'm based near a ranger cabin near Fishing Bridge. My phone is broken, but if you want to meet up, swing by the Fishing Bridge Ranger Station.

Ember

The second I hit "send" on the message, I had that uncomfortable feeling in my stomach again. The one I got when I was feeling something was wrong with me, or my choices, anyway. I thought of Traci mentioning "convictions" and decided yes, that's it; I just didn't know for what. Because how could this have been wrong? Ridge's rejection had hurt my feelings. Sure, he said he wanted to wait until marriage for anything physical. Well, why wasn't he courting me for marriage if he thougt I was so beautiful?

Sure, I'd been behaving a little annoying regarding my phone. But he just didn't understand. I was building my platform. I was working on my enterprise. At one point, I would never have to work again if I just kept posting photos of myself or products on my feed. Talking to Graham wasn't wrong. We had never even met. And if we did meet up by chance during this whirlwind Yellowstone trip, well that was just icing on the cake of this already weird experience.

Still not feeling great about my message to Graham, I reminded myself that I had come here to get Graham's attention. And maybe, to take the attention off of Nicollette and her expensive trip to Africa. This was always the plan. But then my thoughts went to Ridge. Masculine, chivalrous Ridge, who gave up his own bed in his perfect woodsy little cabin so that I could sleep comfortably. And now, I was messaging other men on the internet. Even if nothing happened with Ridge in the end, Graham was only going to muddy the waters of the feelings that I was developing. *Oh, Lord,* I prayed. *How did I go so wrong?*

Graham, I know I just told you to come here. But plans have changed. I'm actually not going to be here anymore, and I'm leaving the park right now. Have a good trip.

Ember

Relief washed over me. I would have to catch up with Graham another time. Perhaps this got the ball rolling for a future rendezvous, but for now, the icky, uncomfortable feeling had subsided in my gut. I did some more scrolling on social media and saw that not much had been happening the last few days. No bombshell posts, no exciting new brand deals in my inbox. Nicollette herself had been very quiet in Africa, only posting a photo of a heart drawn in red dirt in her stories.

Suddenly, Ridge pulled back up to the station. It was nearly five o'clock, and I quickly logged out and closed the browser.

"Hi," I said, cheerfully. "How was it?" Ridge met my eyes and smiles in return.

"She's not quite back yet. Must have taken a detour. I'm going to wait until she's in the boundaries before I go out again, as that was a two-hour round trip for nothing. I knew better, considering her radio collar hasn't pinged near me yet," he laughed under his breath, riding the high that nature seemed to give him. "And how did it go with the camera?" he asked.

"Oh, the camera? Good. I got some pictures in. I'll get them loaded on the computer shortly and be done with it." I looked back to the chair I was sitting in, but the camera wasn't there. Where did I set it down? Then, I saw it: My eyes widened in horror as I realized I set the camera on top of the wood stove and the plastic had melted, surely destroying the camera in its wake.

Ridge's eyes saw it the same time I did. I waited for him to freak out, as I was internally, especially after that big speech I gave him about being good with technology. I covered my mouth and let out a small scream under my breath.

"I'm SO sorry, Ridge! Let me make it up to you—I will buy you a new camera!" I pleaded again, as I had just hours ago, but this time it was for forgiveness. Though with my purse in the wreckage of my car, and my limited funds even if I had my purse, I didn't know how I would. But this was owed to him.

"You don't have to do that, Ember." Ridge's voice had a softness to it that made me feel worse.

"Of course I do. You didn't want me to use it, but I begged you to, and now look! I've ruined it!" He shook his head.

"This is my fault. I knew better, and this is the consequence. It's okay, Ember. I forgive you."

"It is NOT okay, Ridge. Please, just like get mad at me or something." He picked up the camera from the wood stove where it was starting to look like a Salvador Dali painting and turned to me.

"Why would you want me to get mad at you?" His eyes squinted in confusion. He pulled the memory card out of the melted wreckage and found that it was still intact.

"Because I deserve it."

"Have you ever heard of grace, Ember?" Ridge's words sounded soft like pillows coming out of his mouth, with not a sliver of anger in them. Now, he was speaking in riddles.

"I knew her in middle school. She played the trumpet and had rainbow-colored braces. What about her?" I crossed my arms.

"Ha," he said, shaking his head. "Good one. I don't mean grace as in a person. I mean it as a far-generous gift that God has extended to all of us by giving us forgiveness, compassion, and most importantly, salvation, when we don't deserve it. We can't earn it, either. We just have to accept it."

CHAPTER 22
GOD HAS A WAY OF INTERRUPTING
RIDGE

Tracking Raya was thrilling. Though I only could get live updates while I was at the computer in the ranger station, where a beautiful woman was waiting for me to return, I was riding the high of being out in the field. I knew I was leaving my base too soon—the chances of seeing Raya's re-entry was slim as it was, and I should have just waited for her to be back inside the boundaries to see where she went. But I needed time to think about what happened today, and being in nature was my greatest time spent with God.

Ember was complicated. Immature at times. Easily wounded. She reminded me of some of the girls I went to high school with back in our ranch community. Despite growing up in one of the most beautiful places in the world in the shadow of the mountains along the Gallatin River, they all wanted so much more out of life. Lights, cameras, fancy red carpets and things.

More attention than any one person could ever give them. All but one of those girls eventually left Montana, and I'd no clue where they went to , but I prayed they had found what they were looking for.

For Ember, she grew up in a city, and she was vacationing in nature. I couldn't help but feel hopeful that perhaps she would fall in love with nature as I had, but my gut was telling me I needed to pray. So, I did. And God told me the words I didn't ever want to hear, but words I would honor and respect with all of my being: *I need to wait.*

There was something about Ember I couldn't shake, despite her challenges. *God, am I just transfixed by her beauty?* I asked in prayer, but an answer didn't come right away.

My radio went off in my truck; it was Travis giving a report about a hiker who sprained their ankle at the Fairy Falls trailhead. "Right as she got out of her car, she rolled it by stepping on a loose rock. I'm taking her to the medical building." Hmm. Seems like someone was helping a woman in need, as he had criticized me for doing before. I couldn't hold back my smile.

As I drove through the winding road to where it looked like Raya might have re-entered, my eyes were cast upon the endless acres of pine forests in the distance. Nearly every other tree was standing upright, but dead, thanks to the pine beetle infestation in the Shoshone National Forest.

Having the dead trees surrounding the healthy trees felt like a recipe for disaster. I considered the things in my own life that mimicked this scenario and once again, I prayed. *God, has my passion for the wilderness brought me to Yellowstone or was it always my quest for a wife? Am I here for the right reasons or am I trying to rush You?* Of course, the first woman I met I felt serendipity about. I let out a long sigh. *God, please guard my heart and don't let my eagerness allow me to have feelings that You don't intend. I very much want to save all of these things for my future wife.*

My mind went back again to our near-kiss this afternoon. Had I had no self-control, I would have gone through with it. Heck, every fiber of my being wanted to kiss her perfect lips from the moment I saw her, and I felt my face getting hot at the thought of it. I had told her how I felt about it, too. Suddenly, our exchange felt like a secret that I would keep. While there were a few women I had kissed in my younger years, I dedicated my life to Christ out of high school, and this had been one of my greatest convictions ever since: to save all forms of physical intimacy for my future wife. No, it had not been easy. And it wasn't due to a lack of offers from women, either, which had added to its pressure, especially as I was in my mid-twenties. I felt like I was in my prime of life. I had both the energy and the time to get to know someone. All I needed was God to send the right one.

After a few hours of wolf-watching, my mind became increasingly unsettled. I felt like I needed to return to the station. On one hand, I felt drawn to Ember in ways I'd never felt before with any woman. But again, could that just have been my eagerness to marry? As I turned the key in the ignition to head back, I prayed that God would remind me that I was on His timetable, not my own. All of these things I had known in my heart. But living them, while I was in the company of a beautiful woman, was certainly making itself out to be more of a challenge.

Returning back to the ranger station, my heart quickened its pace. I saw Ember sitting at the computer through the windows. No doubt, she was doing whatever it was she needed to do for her work. Though I couldn't relate in any way, shape, or form, I respected that she had built something on her own that she needed to nurture.

Entering the station, I caught the scent of something melting. After greeting Ember, both of our eyes went to the camera. She apologized profusely, and I felt disappointment, as I would need to ask for a replacement, but I was not mad. Getting angry over an accident was futile, even if it was done in carelessness. Truthfully, it didn't matter to me what happened, and I was more concerned at this moment that she felt so terrible about it.

Growing up on the ranch, when I made a mistake, my dad would let me sit in my feelings for as long as I needed to. I remembered once I accidentally left a gate open in an area where we didn't have a cattle guard to prevent them from leaving. About two dozen of them had left the area and headed for a neighbor's ranch, and one had gotten injured on the way by a sharp piece of barbed wire. That cow, Gertie, had to wear a little bandage on her leg for a week. Every time I looked at her, I felt bad because if I had just closed the gate, she wouldn't have needed to feel that pain. She wouldn't have needed the little leg wrap.

My father extended continuous forgiveness on me, just like the Lord does for everyone who seeks it. He never got mad at me, even when sometimes I thought it would be easier.

Instead, he showed me how to deal with the consequences of my actions because we all fail. We all make mistakes. But thanks to our God, we can recover from them if we seek His forgiveness and wisdom. When I told this to Ember, her expression told me that she, too, like I had felt as a child, would rather I had just been upset with her.

But I was not upset. I knew the moment I gave the camera, which was something I wasn't supposed to do, that it was on me now if anything happened. And it did.

"I'm just so sorry," she whispered.

"No need, Ember. You didn't mean to do it. I know what that feels like." I hoped my words resonated with her, as I certainly did know well how that felt. In this case, I was Gertie the cow, and the camera was my leg wound. I wanted to hug her at that moment like my dad hugged me, but I held back. This was Ember's journey to navigate. I did not know the plans that God had for her at this time, and I didn't want to muddy up the waters with a hug that, let's face it, would have meant a heck of a lot more to me than just being friendly. Until my head was cleared, it was crucial that we kept things in the friend zone only, with no boundaries being crossed.

*****

That evening, Ember and I shared the rest of the chili, warmed up over the campfire. Her guard was up but slowly softening. We talked about idle things; mostly enjoying the warmth of the flames. Ember seemed pretty out of it and announced she was heading off to bed.

"Goodnight, Ember," I said, our eyes only meeting for a moment. "I'll be here when you wake up." She nodded.

The next morning, I rose early, just as I usually did. I had coffee bubbling over the flames of the campfire—two scents that I didn't think I could ever truly tire of. As I waited for Ember to rise, I considered a few things, when I contemplated today being my day off. First, Ember came to Yellowstone for an adventure—one that she certainly got, but not in a good way. Secondly, my job was to be a steward of all of the things in the park. It would be good to spend today taking in the sites, to refamiliarize myself with everything the park had to offer. Lastly, I didn't know when Raya would return, but it wasn't imperative that I saw her re-entry. Her collar would make it known that she was here, and from there, if luck and God were on my side, I would see her at some point.

When Ember finally emerged from my small log cabin quarters, my decision was cemented. There were a few sites that I wanted to show her today, so she could understand my love for this area and God's creation. The woman looked like she needed some cheering up and Lord knows, distraction from her phone, with all directions pointing to God.

"Good morning, Ember. Here is some coffee," I said, standing to rise as she came out.

"Thank you. If only I had someone at home doing this." She giggled about the coffee tasting much better when someone else made it. I waited for her to drink her mug while mulling over the route I would be taking us on—if she was up for it, anyway. When I noticed her unusable phone was sticking out of her sweatpants' pocket, like it might have turned on at any minute, I felt the need to pray for her.

"How about we go on a little adventure today?" I asked, smiling ear to ear. She looked at me like I was from another planet.

"My feet are kind of starting to hurt." She pointed to her very new-looking hiking shoes. I nodded.

"That's a rough road ahead for you, to break in new boots, I'm afraid. But what do you say for a little fun to distract you from your foot pain?" She took the bait, nodding in agreement.

"Okay, why not. It's not like I have anywhere else I need to be. Besides, that wrecker is going to call before he comes, right?"

"Yes. We won't miss him." And with that, she went inside to change back into her hiking outfit that I met her in, which looked great on her and showed off her tanned legs. It took every cell in my body, extraordinary strength, not to check her out, but slowly and with much prayer, I started to overcome my temptation to do so.

CHAPTER 23
THE BEST THINGS AREN'T CURATED
EMBER

Ridge wouldn't give me any hints to where we were off to, but instead, every time I asked, he just said "trust me." As if I didn't already! In fact, I had from the moment we met. When my life was in complete danger during the microburst, I had jumped into his arms. It wasn't lost on me that I prayed in that moment, before Ridge appeared. The longer I was here, without my phone, the quieter the world was getting. If only I could have quieted down the pull I had to my dead phone. As of now, I was still carrying it around like it might have just grown a mouth and communicated with me. I was rivaling delusion, but it was proving hard to overcome.

Ridge expertly took the curves of the road ahead, avoiding all of the potholes that came into our lane. I started to relax for the first time in—I don't even know how long—but as

I was enjoying the beautiful scenery, he turned into a parking area.

"First stop—the mud pots," he said with a grin that rivaled the morning sun.

"What now? A mud *pot?*" The imagery that had come to mind was the large stew pot my mother had used when I was growing up to make split pea soup and other things that I never had enjoyed eating. Now, it sounded pretty good to have my mom make me a home cooked meal.

"You'll see," Ridge said, and I waited for him to come open my door, knowing that either way he would, so I might as well have let him.

"Why the uniform—I thought it was your day off?" I asked him, noticing that he was still wearing all of his contraband.

"I'm still here to help. I'm just not getting paid today," he winked, and with that, he closed the door behind me, and we started our first adventure of the day.

Every place he took me to was a greater adventure than the last. I smelled some foul geysers, walked so far, I thought my feet might have fallen off, and saw colors I could only imagine would be in the skies of heaven. As we summited the upward trail at the Grand Prismatic Spring overlook, the shock crossed my mind. How could something so beautiful, so wild and stunning, exist? While Ridge handed me a water canteen, I felt tears well in my eyes at the sight of the spring. Getting up here had been quite the battle—heck, being in Yellowstone had been the most challenging time of my life, but Ridge was right—this was the exact kind of experience I had needed.

As we neared the lunch hour, we stopped at a picnic table overlooking a scenic lake. A small family was there, enjoying the wooded area as their children played in the water of the lake shore.

"Do you want a family of your own?" I asked, as I gazed upon the cute children enjoying the simple pleasures of splashing each other.

"Yes. If it is God's will, I would love to have that." I smiled at the answer. Once again, Ridge was showing me what it meant to live a Christ-centered life. If only I could've figured out how to live that way. "What about you?" he asked, as he took a bite of one of the sandwiches we picked up at a General Store nearby.

"I've never really thought about it," I said. "Honestly, I've spent most of my life thinking about myself and nothing—

or no one—else." The words felt frustrating to say, but once I did, I felt relief. As if I brought my shame out of the darkness, and it no longer had anywhere to hide. Ridge just listened. And at that moment, it was like the floodgates opened. Things just started to roll off my lips, and I couldn't stop them.

Before I knew it, I had told him about Traci and how I had treated that friendship over the last several years. I had been a terrible friend. I told him about my parents, always bailing me out. I shared with him about my failures in life in general and at the very last moment of our picnic table conversation, I had realized something else.

"I shouldn't have children. I would probably mess that up, too," I said. The self-deprecating was in full blast now, and I couldn't figure out how to turn things around. But Ridge was a generous, kind man, and he knew just what to say.

"After hearing about all the things you regret, which I understand, you have a few options." Options? What was he talking about? "You see the wrong, and you want to correct it. Right?" I nodded profusely.

"I want nothing more than to fix these things," I pleaded.

"Here's the good news: you can. And I think you know just what to do." I agreed. I knew I needed to make it up to my family and Traci. But Ridge continued. "Secondly, just the growth you've had being here for a few days, away from the hustle and bustle, tells me that you are still evolving. You will still be for some time, I think. Don't be so hard on yourself. If God can forgive you of your mistakes, you need to accept His love and grow from it. It's never too late to change. And it's not God who wants you to replay your regrets all day." I weighed on his words for a moment, before snapping back, lightening the mood in the process.

"Evolving is a very kind way to say I have some maturing to do, Ridge." We both laughed as I called out the elephant in the room.

"Ready for our next stop on this adventure?" he asked, standing up. His generosity in listening to my failures but graciously sharing what he thought and the love that God had for me, built me up. I was starting to see how God had brought me here for a reason because this was the only way He could get a hold of me. It was not lost on me that without my cell phone, while feeling the most disconnected I'd ever felt in my life, I was starting to discover something real.

*****

Waterfalls. Hummingbirds. Swans. Rainbow pools. Bison. Rock chucks. Steaming geysers. Elk. A tiny chipmunk wielding a pinecone twice its size. I'd seen more beauty today than I'd ever had in my life. Our last stop of the day was to watch Old Faithful erupt. And as we waited for it to blow, we chatted with excitement as a little boy came over to Ridge, dressed head to toe in a cowboy outfit.

"Excuse me, mister," he piped up, looking up at Ridge and holding onto his small cowboy hat. "Do you like being a park ranger?" His question was so contemplated, so serious, that my heart melted. Ridge leaned down, trying to get to the young boy's level. The child's parents stood behind him.

"Yes, sir, I do. Do you want to know why?" The little boy nodded in eager anticipation. "Because I get to see fierce grizzly bears and big, hairy buffalo walk around in the wilds of the outdoors. Doesn't that sound fun?" The little cowboy's eyes widened, and he grinned, ear to ear, just like Ridge had earlier when he was talking about this impending adventure. Ridge, and perhaps this child, was born with a zeal for the outdoors. For nature. For all things that are *real.* I realized then, I wanted that. I wanted to be doing things that mattered. Did anything I did matter? The all-too common feeling of regret washed over me again.

Ridge had said something before about regret, implying that replaying our regrets over and over was the devil's work. At least, that's what I got from it. I started to wonder about the devil, or "the enemy," as I'd heard Traci refer to him. Suddenly, a thought took my mind captive: All of my distractions, if they were keeping me from God, could they be from Satan? At first, the thought seemed ridiculous, and I laughed. Watching Ridge talk to the parents of the small child, shaking their hands, he turned back to me. He asked me what was so funny.

"I just had the craziest thought," I said, putting my palm to my forehead.

"Oh yeah? Go for it," he said, putting his hands in his pockets.

"That all of my distractions—phone, TV, radio, you name it—are from the devil. Ha!" Ridge gave me a very serious look.

"In this case, Ember, it could very well be. I mean... If the devil's goal is to keep us from knowing the one true God, he is going to use whatever tool he can get his hands on—whatever works for people—to distract you from Him." My jaw dropped.

"So, do you think that God gave me that thought just now?" My words turned into a whisper. He nodded.

"It sounds like you're on the right path, Ember." He put his hands on my shoulders, and briefly, we shared a wonderful amount of eye contact. This time, I didn't shy away. Then suddenly, a loud noise went off, and Ridge moved out of the way so I could see Old Faithful in all of her glory.

CHAPTER 24
THE WILD TESTS WHO YOU ARE
RIDGE

After a long and exhausting day that ended with a stroll through the historic Old Faithful Lodge, I could tell Ember was worn out.

"What do you say we get out of here? The fire pit outside of my cabin is calling my name, and I have a bag of marshmallows that pair really well with steak." Her eyes lit up at my suggestion.

"I'd like that."

Back at my cabin, I opened the door and held it open with a river rock. If we were both going to be inside of this somewhat secluded set of walls, I wanted the door to remain open, to cloud any question of funny business if someone were to happen upon us. Silly, I knew, but a woman's reputation was everything.

I pulled two steaks out of the fridge that I had thawed earlier in the week, planning to eat them on different nights, but

I was so thankful there were two. Seasoning them on each side, the plump steaks smelled heavenly, and I grabbed my cast iron and put it outside on the grate that sat just inside of the flames. As it heated, I added some pure butter to the pan, throwing on the steaks when it was hot enough. The sizzles and fragrances made my mouth water.

"Is that rosemary?" Ember asked behind me, taking a deep breath to smell it.

"Of course. I can't think of a better scent, either."

"Rosemary and garlic are my go-to spices. I eat pretty clean, and boy do they dress up a bland diet." Her laughter was enriching to hear, and the mood was lifting every second.

"What does clean eating mean to you?" I, of course, knew what it meant to me—no franken-foods from a factory. These marshmallows I had were hand-tooled from a family back home even. You could still enjoy treats that weren't completely garbage.

"It means no fattening foods when I can reasonably avoid them. I eat a lot of protein bars and supplements like that. My favorite are these protein pastries. Oh, how I'm craving one right now! I have a crazy sweet tooth, and sometimes that gets the better of me. Like the promise of those marshmallows earlier? All I can think about." I grinned ear to ear, nodding as I got up.

"A little dessert before dinner never hurt anyone that I know of." I retrieved the bag out of the cabin and found a proper, straight stick, breaking off the branches on it that weren't needed. "Here you go." I handed her the stick and the marshmallows, and she squealed like a kid in a candy store.

"Thank you!" Her excitement was contagious, and before I could even flip the steaks, I found myself reaching in the bag for one, too.

"Mmm."

"You're not going to toast it?" She was turning her stick like a hot dog oven at a gas station.

"I probably should, but they are just irresistible as is. A family near our ranch back home makes baked goods of all kinds, and these are my favorite. They even sell some of their products here at the general stores."

"That's it! You're telling me that these are your favorite? I can't wait any longer." As Ember pulled her marshmallow out of the fire, it was encompassed in flames. Blowing on it, she extinguished the blaze and promptly put it up to her lips before pulling it away. "And it's seven thousand degrees at the moment." I watched her shake it around and wave it through the air to cool it like an artist sculpting a palette, completely mesmerized by her movements. Finally, after a prolonged interpretive dance with her marshmallow roasting stick, she bit into the marshmallow and experienced all of its gooey glory.

"Well?" I asked, my eyebrows raised expectantly while she chewed the sticky confection.

"You were right about one thing," she said.

"What's that?"

"This couldn't hurt anyone. I feel renewed from the sugar." She grinned; the residue of the marshmallow was all over her hands, and she tossed the stick aside. "I better wash up. Everything is sticky now. How did that happen? I don't even think I touched it with my hands." Her laughter carried through the woods and was the perfect companion to the chirping grasshoppers and short bursts of wind that howled above us. As the night fell and I saw the first few stars checker the sky, my heart felt full. *God, I will wait for whatever it is You have, just as You told me to.*

*****

The night's conversation over dinner was one for the books. Ember's personality was starting to reveal itself more with every moment and for the first time since I'd known her, she didn't seem to care about not having her phone right beside her.

After the steaks were gone, Ember remarked about the stars in the sky. Just as we both looked up, a shooting star flew by, making quite the romantic moment between us. Honoring what I promised God, I didn't let the moment cloud my mind or judgment, but I couldn't say for certain how Ember felt.

"Wow," she said, with a slight sadness in her voice. The feelings of earlier creeping back in my mind. I knew she felt rejected initially about me not kissing her, but I gave her the knowledge of my *wanting* to do so, and I hoped that might have been enough for her.

"It's pretty magical out here, isn't it?" With nothing around to artificially light up the sky, the stars were so bright, they looked like lightbulbs. The moon, in its crescent waning phase, gently illuminated the creek that ran through the area to our left. A coyote could be heard howling in the distance. Ember shuddered at the noise.

"Are we safe out here?" Her voice creaked as she spoke.

"Yes. The coyotes want little to do with us. But I bet they would love to lick these plates clean," I said, retrieving our dishes and putting them inside in the small kitchen sink. I returned with an oven mitt so I could grab the cast iron out of the fire, taking it inside and setting it on the small two-burner stove. When I turned back around, Ember was right behind me; the door still ajar behind us.

"I got scared out there." The space between us was slim, not even a foot of air in the small void. Instinctively, I took a step to the side, making it appear as natural as I could.

"I understand that," I said, turning again and putting the oven mitt back in the small drawer next to the oven. Though she didn't touch me, I could feel her shift in the room. She was close enough to me that if I moved a hair, our bodies would meet.

"Want another marshmallow?" she said, reaching into the bag that I didn't notice she had held before. I nodded, thinking it would take us outside and out of this small proximity challenge, and I turned. There she was, a handful of inches between us, holding up another marshmallow to reach my lips.

"I'm sorry, Ember. I can't do this, and I thought I made that clear before." I held my hands up in defeat, but I felt immobilized.

"Do what? Accept a marshmallow?" The rejection was written all over her face. I put my hands down and instead, took one of hers. Her entire face perked up as I led her back outside to the fire. I sat down, and she followed, in her same spot she was sitting before, across from me. I sighed in relief.

"Look, Ember. I don't want this to come off the wrong way, because I'm very *tempted* by you. To have the chance to kiss such a beautiful woman as yourself is truly a gift, I'm sure. But I have my reasons to abstain." She nodded, sadly.

"Yeah, yeah. Your future wife. But why can't that be me?" Her words rocked my core—sure, this woman was bold, but I didn't see that coming.

"I never said it couldn't. But I am working on a different timetable here." My thoughts were scrambling; I'd pictured talking about things like this for years but now that I was forced to verbalize it, I was coming up short.

"And what timetable is that? Because it's established that we are both very attracted to each other, which is the basis for any relationship." She smirked.

"I'm on God's timing." Her smile fell as she nodded. "And I disagree with one thing." She looked at me intensely and at this moment, I felt like a stranger in my own skin talking. "Attraction is important, sure. But God is the basis of a marriage. And though my attraction to you has been interesting to explore, I am not sure yet if God ordains it." It was hard to say the words out loud. I didn't say them as thoughtfully as I could have. I didn't intend to be so brash. Ember looked away, a small tear falling down her cheek as her brightly colored nails flashed when she wiped it away.

"In that case," she whispered, which felt more like a prayer.

"I'm sorry, I didn't mean that to sound so... final." Her eyes remained on the fire, not looking at me as I spoke like she had before. I had hurt her feelings. "I'm not saying there is not a chance for us. I just don't want to do anything until we both know for certain if there is." She slowly nodded as the wind picked up, bringing in a cool breeze with it.

"So, what. You and your future wife will just stare at the trees for entertainment?" she asked.

"And the stars. Don't forget we have millions of those to name." I winked, but the moment between us was turning sour, so I felt like nothing I could say would change it.

"I'm super tired. Is it alright if I head to bed? I can take the sleeping bag in the truck bed, if you want your own bed back." I quickly nodded.

"No, thank you. I sleep better out here. I've got a pad that my sleeping bag goes on, so it's actually quite comfortable." She nodded and looked at me one more time with her tearful eyes. This was the second time she'd cried today, but this time, it was because of something I'd said. And that just didn't work for me. "May I walk you to the cabin?" She nodded and stood. As we took the five steps required, I pulled the river rock away from the door and held it open as she walked inside. "Goodnight, Ember. I'm praying that God gives us both the clarity we need, as I do want to kiss you." And with that, her eyes lit up, and we both felt complete.

CHAPTER 25
WOLVES, WONDER, AND A CHANGED HEART
EMBER

That night, I wrestled with my feelings of rejection, but instead of being hurt, I felt like Ridge was right. He *wanted* to kiss me. To explore the idea of a life with me. He was interested. But his reasoning was completely new territory to me. I'd never once in my life met a man who wasn't controlled by his lusts—taking any chance to kiss a woman—and here's Ridge, who was instead doing everything in his power to be the opposite.

I had a hard time sleeping. But this time, instead of checking my dead phone every few minutes, that, surprise—I still didn't have a charging cord for—it was because of that ill feeling in my gut.

In all of my life, I'd never once felt conviction for anything that wasn't fashion or aesthetic related. The only things I'd ever felt with all of my being were related to desires of things I wanted to purchase or do—all of which were completely selfish endeavors. I couldn't even recall a time when I thought of what anyone else might want or need. And now, as I was stranded in the middle of God's most glorious creation, I was more worried about appealing to a man than my God. Ridge was right—he said it as gently as he could, but I had some maturing to do.

Sometime in the middle of the night, when I was certain I'd been tossing and turning for hours, I finally cried out to God. For real this time. I went to Him with my emotional baggage, my sins, my mistakes, and He took them off of me. I finally committed my life to Him, and He carried the weight of my burdens, so I no longer had to. And finally, He showed me what I needed to do. And that would be started immediately.

I woke up from a brief sleep early; the sun was casting a pre-dawn glow through the little pane windows of the log cabin. I promptly rose, washed my face, and readied for the day. I rounded up the few things I owned and put them in the bag that Ridge had my fresh clothes in. When I went outside, I wasn't surprised that Ridge was already up, making coffee at the crackling fire.

"Good morning," I said, expecting to alarm him that I was up already. Instead, he smiled.

"How did you sleep?" he asked, holding a cup of coffee out to me. I accepted it, sitting at the other side of the fire and taking in all the glorious smells of Yellowstone: pine trees, dirt, and wildflowers, plus the scent of this heavenly roast of coffee.

"I am reborn," I said, looking at Ridge sheepishly to see if he picked up on anything. He stared back at me with wonder but just nodded. We sat for a while in silence, mulling over the words that could be said, but neither one spoke. Eventually, he retrieved a pot from inside and made oatmeal with fresh milk, foraged berries, and honey that came from a Mason jar. It was as real as food got, and I was so appreciative of having a glimpse into this life. This way of living without being chained to a phone wasn't just an experience. I was starting to feel like it was the way that God intended for all of us.

As the fire died down, Ridge announced that he was ready to go report to the station if I was. I nodded. There was something I needed to do.

When we arrived, Travis was there. He didn't say much, but he smiled at both of us, which was a huge improvement.

"How did your hiker with the rolled ankle recover?" Ridge asked him, to which Travis just smiled. "I see." Travis announced he was going to check on her now and left.

"Would it be okay if I made a few phone calls this morning? I don't want to interrupt your workday any more than I already have this week." I felt remorseful for the camera and all of the other things he'd had to do to put up with me.

"Absolutely. I will step outside while you do." And when Ridge graciously did, I thought about that word again: grace. We couldn't earn it, and we didn't deserve it, but we could accept it. Finally, I did.

The call I was about to make was going to be hard. But there was no avoiding it any longer.

"Mom?" I asked as she answered the phone.

"Hi, sweetie. How's Yellowstone? Still no phone, huh?"

"No, no phone. There is more to the story, actually. A lot more. For one, my car was crushed by a tree." Her gasp was followed by a peppering of questions. "I'm okay. I was spared. But there's even more." I paused, starting again. "Secondly, everything was inside, including my wallet. I'm stranded here, but the park... The personnel have been very gracious in assisting me." I told her the whole story and at the end, she was in tears herself. "Please don't be mad at me. I know you and Dad stuck your neck out to help me get that car. I've made some royal mistakes along the way, and I'm coming to terms with my phone and social media addiction. Lastly, I've committed my life to Christ, and if I can ever get out of here, I am ready to show you that I'm going to be following His path for my life very seriously."

"Ember, how could I ever feel anger towards you? I'm your mom. Sure, there are things that are frustrating in life, but a tree falling on my sweet daughter's car and her not being inside of it is a miracle. Not a cause for anger." I let out the breath I'd been holding in.

"Thank you. I just want you to know, I'm sorry for all the things I've been selfish about in my life. I've been living for myself and not thinking about anyone else—and certainly, not Jesus. That's changing now." I heard tears of joy on the other end of the line.

"I'm so proud of you, dear. Now, let's get you home." We spent several minutes coordinating a pickup location for a shuttle that she found online, placing me on hold every time she spoke with them. The wrecker had already been arranged, and when my mom asked by whom, I just gave her a vague answer.

"One of the park rangers here called the tow company for me."

"Uh huh," she said, with a smile behind her voice.

"It looks like, if we can get you to Cody, Wyoming, there's a direct flight to Denver every day. You could be back here as soon as tonight." The heat rose to my cheeks as my gaze moved towards the window and at Ridge outside. As much as I knew it was time to leave, there were things that I wished I didn't have to leave behind. Ridge was a wonderful man and would make a woman very happy someday. If I hadn't been so selfish, immature, and erratic, maybe that could have been me. I remembered something Traci used to say about trusting God with your dating life and smiled. *Here I am, God. I'm giving it all to You.*

When I was done with my phone calls, I stuck my head outside. "I'm all done." Ridge was in his truck, tooling with something inside.

"Okay. Perfect timing—I need to check something on the computer." He did just that, letting out a low whistle when he opened a map screen with a small, red, moving circle. "She's back."

"Raya?" I asked, my heart full of wonder.

"Yes. There she is. Just an hour away. Her den was over here, so I imagine if I head towards it now, I will see her when she returns. And see what she returned for." His words were full of excitement. Excitement that was contagious. "Would you like to go with me?" he turned and asked, his eyes sparkling.

With regret, I shook my head. "I would love to. But as much as it pains me to say no, I need to stay. I have organized transportation home today, and they will be here sometime this afternoon." His face fell as I spoke.

"Already?" he asked, which felt more like a question to God than me.

"Yes. It's time, Ridge. But thank you for your hospitality. I couldn't have survived without you."

"Is it because of something I said?" he asked.

"No, not like that. What you did was lead me to some personal convictions that were a long time coming. God has got it from here, and I thank you." Ridge's eyes widened and for a second, I saw something new in his eyes: hope. He quickly wiped that look away.

"What time did you say they were coming?" He looked at his watch.

"The car service said they could be here this afternoon, but won't know until they get closer, since their exact route isn't clear. They said there are still some major landslides on the road to Cody, and the highway in Livingston, Montana, the other direction, is shut down for wind speeds. It's some seriously wild weather out there."

"They must be coming from Billings, Montana?" he asked, and I nodded. "Their best bet is to go through Bozeman, but yeah, if that freeway is closed... Either way, I think we have some time." He clasped his hands together.

"Time for what?"

"For you to see Raya... with me. It's not even eight yet. If we leave now, we could be back by one, if you're comfortable with that margin of time, that is." I threw caution to the wind and agreed, trusting Ridge wouldn't lead me astray.

The minutes in the truck went by like seconds as I was whisked away on an adventure. I knew Ridge was a cautious but exact driver, though I was certain in some parts of the trip we were speeding, but I didn't care; there was so much beauty to be seen just from the road. Colorful geyser ponds with bubbling waters. Herds of bison with their babies, to which Ridge referred to them as "red dogs." The further we drove, I started to see more life; rivers with swans floating, streams with fisherman, and mountain lakes with people paddling canoes. The early morning had rivaled the adventures of yesterday afternoon. All of that and more. But the greatest of all, was for once in my life,

I had chosen to savor an experience, focusing on God, rather than feeding my phone addiction.

Admitting I had an addiction to my phone was important. Deep down, I'd always known. Those around me had known. Traci had been hinting at it for years but had I ever listened to anyone? No. And that pained me. I'd wasted a lot of time in my life, but I was ready to turn a new leaf. As I thought these thoughts, I looked over to my left at Ridge. He was such a hunk of a man, and one who wanted to save himself—all of him—for marriage. Though we were close in age, I could see the stark difference in our maturity. The difference in our goals and connections. To have thought that I had been trying to foil that this week was disheartening. But that had been my old life. I was now thinking of others—Ridge had inspired me.

I had yearned to connect with people I didn't know and would likely never meet. Ridge wanted more Jesus, to the point of turning away from his own wants. I didn't understand it at first, but now I saw it: We were not the same. But Lord willing, God would work on my heart. He would move the mountains of my desires and align them for the things that brought Him glory, not my own.

Just thinking these thoughts let me know that God was truly with me, because never before had I thought anything remotely close to this. Ever since I had gotten a phone at thirteen and a social media account, my life had been for the world. My parents had been moderately involved but never had considered any of it might have been harmful to me. But in the end, it was all on me, not them. I had been the only one responsible for my actions. And now, I laid them at the feet of Jesus.

CHAPTER 26
THE DAY I FORGOT TO MISS MY PHONE
EMBER

Ridge pulled onto a dirt road, jumping out to open the gate. It was marked for park personnel only. We slowed down, as the road was deep with mud.

"I hope we don't get stuck in this mud. Your wrecker might have to come pull me out, too." I felt a twinge in my heart as I remembered my car was destroyed, racking my brain for ideas on what to do about it. Hopefully, my car insurance would cover the loss, because I still had a loan on it. A loan that my parents had co-signed. They were going to be so unimpressed. Depression took over my mind as I was once again humbled by it.

"I'm sorry for being such a drag on your week," I said to Ridge, finally. His eyes widened.

"Who said this has been anything but fun?" I shrugged.

"I don't know. I'm just in my feelings for the first time in... my life." I put my hand to my forehead, trying to ward off the tears that were now rising to the surface. "I'm just ready to start all over. Nothing I've done up until this point has been sustainable. God is showing me all of this and more." The mud in the road turned to dirt as we came out of the trees, and Ridge came to a stop, shifting the truck into park.

"You can start over anytime you want, Ember, by going to Jesus. He will make your paths straight." Ridge had no fear, no doubt or shame in his voice. I'd yet to manage being confident about anything on this topic, despite having heard about Jesus my whole life. For some reason, it had been an uncomfortable topic to discuss. But I wanted to change that. Now.

"Thank you, Ridge. You've inspired me to do that. And I did. Last night. I committed my life to Him. Now, I'm dealing with the aftermath of my actions that are known to the world." Ridge's eyes softened as I spoke. He reached his hand out, as if he was going to hold mine, but stopped short. Our hands were next to each other, and neither one of us moved them closer. It was enough just to have him near me.

"There's nothing you can't come back from, Ember. That's the point." He smiled, and as he did, the clouds broke, revealing a warm glow on my face. As if God was shining down on me.

"Thank You, Jesus," I whispered, feeling the warmth of the Holy Spirit. The intimacy of this moment was something I'd never experienced before. Ridge and I sat in silence for a few minutes, before he unbuckled his seatbelt.

"I'm going to check this scene out. You want to join me?" I nodded. I didn't come all this way to sit in the truck, but now that it was time, I wished I had brought a jacket... Not that I had one. The weather here was so tumultuous. Hard to believe that when I had arrived, I was wearing shorts. Now, for the last few days, I'd been rotating between a hiking outfit and a gift shop sweatsuit.

"Let's go," I said, and before I could even get unbuckled, Ridge was out of the truck and opening my door. The best part? He reached in his back seat and retrieved two jackets, handing me one. I put it on immediately, feeling the warmth comfort my bones.

There's a little bit of a hike involved. "If these boots aren't broken in by now, I'm writing the manufacturer a letter," I said, as I was huffing and puffing. Suddenly, the coat felt heavy, and I was on the verge of overheating. Ridge was comfortably gaining elevation, one step at a time. His legs were longer, and he was stronger, and even though he was going at a snail's pace, I was fighting for my life to keep up with him. For some reason, this hike felt harder than the vertical ascent we had made yesterday at Grand Prismatic Spring.

"It's not too much further. See that rock out there?" He pointed to a boulder by another road. I nodded because I couldn't catch my breath to speak. "We're just going there. There's an overlook of Lamar Valley where we will see if we can spot her." The excitement in his voice was palpable. He pulled out a bag of trail mix and handed it to me. "I know how much you like granola. How about some trail mix?"

I gleefully took the bag, reaching in for a handful and cramming it into my mouth when he wasn't looking. The delightful blend of raisins, M&M's, peanuts, and crunchy bits gave me the energy to power through, and we made it to the boulder at a sizable incline.

"Thank you. That helped," I grinned, still breathing hard.

"I thought it might. Always helps me. It's my emergency stash," he grinned back. I took a few more bites, picking out just the pieces that I wanted.

"Do they make trail mixes that's just M&M's?"

"Yeah. It's called M&M's." He laughed and pulled out his binoculars that looked longer and more powerful than anything I'd seen at a camp store. They were a different set from what we looked at the grizzlies with.

"Dang. Are we on a safari?" I asked.

"I know; these are a little intense, but check this out. You can see ants moving on the ground." He handed them my way, and I set down the trail mix to grab them. They were heavy to the point where if I was using them, they'd need to be on a tripod or something or my arms would fall off. But when I held them up to my eyes and looked through, I was in awe. Ridge was right; I could see everything.

A large valley below with a river running through it like a snake. Hilly mounds topped with fluffy pine trees that housed birds. A sprawling landscape peppered with sagebrush bushes everywhere that certainly hid rabbits and small animals. A large bison roamed, the sunshine hitting his fur, highlighting his warm breath in the cold morning dew. It was remarkable and the tears returned.

"It's absolutely breathtaking," I said, my hands shaking as I handed back the binoculars. "I've seen lots of nature from a computer screen, but it just doesn't compare to witnessing it in person."

"Now you're speaking my language," he winked, as he reached over to my face and wiped a tear off my cheek. Surprised, I leaned back a little. Not enough to change the mood of the moment, but enough to remember that we were both on different paths. Ridge—he was a good man. Just not the man for me. I was too different. He was too good.

Ridge finally turned away from me, looking back into the binoculars. Other people were around us, in the distance, and I saw we were not the only people here to witness the wildlife this morning.

Ridge let out a gasp. "There she is," he said, under his breath. "Raya is back." He pulled the binoculars away and handed them to me. At first, I shook my head.

"You've been waiting for this."

"I want to share it with you," he said, so I took them and looked.

A stunning, white wolf, with paws as large as a loaf of sourdough bread was pacing through the valley in the distance. "Her den was here," Ridge said, as he moved my binoculars a few degrees so I could see where she was likely traveling to.

Just then, a large, black wolf came out from the area of the den. It was my turn to gasp.

"There's another wolf!" I said, as loud of a whisper as I could manage. Ridge nodded.

"I knew they messed it up somehow. That's why she's back. Wolves mate for life," he said. I was so overwhelmed by the beauty of her story, this animal, that if I had seen a picture of her or heard her story a week ago, I might not have thought twice about it. But now seeing it for myself—the power of love and the lengths an animal went to be reunited with her mate—had the tears flowing again. I handed him back the binoculars as I felt ugly tears coming on.

Even without the binoculars, I could see the black and white wolves moving against the stark, green landscape. They didn't make a sound, at least not that I could hear, but they did touch heads. The language they spoke was that of love. And it was a language I didn't speak, but I hoped to learn one day. When I was mature enough for love and when God sent me someone.

The experience of seeing this reunion was not one that I would ever forget. The drive back was filled with my relishing in the experience, and the beauty, and Ridge making many radio calls from his truck to let everyone know what had happened.

"Her mate was left behind," he said firmly.

"Unfortunately, things like that are rarely taken into account, Ridge." The old man on the other side of the radio had a kind voice. When he was done with his calls, we sat in silence. I leaned my head out the window, feeling the air kiss my face. It dried my tears, and the sun brought me the feeling that I was glowing from within.

God, I pray for a love story like Raya. A love that no matter what comes between us, we return to one another—but only when I'm mature enough to handle it. The drive back went by faster than the drive to Lamar Valley, and before I knew it, we pulled back into the ranger station parking area. No wrecker on site. But there was a fancy e-bike propped up against the log building.

"Whose bike is that?" I asked, feeling weary that someone else was here. Ridge shrugged. Travis did not look like he rode a bike, and it was vaguely familiar to me. And then, it dawned on me: There was only one person whom I'd seen with a black bicycle frame and a bright, blue seat. And his name was Graham Jones.

My heart sunk into my stomach. I told him I was leaving, though it wasn't a fully developed idea at the time. Now,

I actually was! This was so awkward, and once again, I was ashamed of my actions.

I didn't want to get out of the truck. Ridge opened the door for me, but I was stuck inside. "There's something I need to tell you," I said quietly, and he looked at me with squinted eyes

"Okay, shoot." But it was too late. I spotted Graham as he was walking around the other side of the porch of the log building.

CHAPTER 27
FILTERS OFF, WALLS DOWN
EMBER

"Ember Hollis?" he hollered out in a squeaky voice. *Ugh.* Ridge turned to look at the man whom, I was sad to say, that Traci was right about his height. He was shorter than me; I'd guessed he came up to my chin. That was okay though. I had realized I didn't care if a guy I really liked was short. It didn't devalue him as a person. But seeing Graham now, and comparing him side by side with Ridge, I realized I didn't have feelings for Graham. Ridge set the bar so high for a godly man that now, I couldn't imagine being with any other type of guy. Certainly not a social media one like I was. Or, had been.

"Hi, Graham," I said, getting out of the truck slowly. I didn't have a stitch of makeup on, and I was wearing old clothes, ready to face another consequence of my actions.

"Wow," he said, ignoring Ridge's towering presence. "I can't believe I'm finally meeting you face to face." As he spoke,

I couldn't help but notice he was evading eye contact. Something I was very comfortable with, as I'd been doing it myself for years.

"It's nice to meet you. I hope you didn't go too far out of your way because I am just leaving, actually." I turned to look at Ridge, hoping to send him a signal with my eyes that I didn't mean for this to happen. This was not only the wrong time and place, but I was a different person yesterday when I had talked to him. I hoped that Ridge got that message. Either way, I turned back to Graham, ready to wish him well on the rest of his journey.

"I did get your message that you were leaving—yes. But I was hoping to just catch a glimpse of you and see if you were as beautiful in person as you are online." A week ago, the words out of his mouth would have been welcomed. Now, I had a bad taste in mine.

"Oh, well, alright then. Really, I must be going." A large engine could be heard shifting from a few yards away. As the wrecker turned into the campground nearby, I let out a bated breath. *Thank You, Lord.*

"You really are just as pretty. I mean, I didn't expect you to dress like this or—you wear makeup normally, yes?" Graham was so tone deaf that I didn't even feel bad for him coming all this way now.

"Ember doesn't even need makeup to look beautiful." Ridge spoke looking right at me. Our eyes locked, and I knew he felt that this situation was unwanted. He continued. "She can wear sweatpants and have her hair in a messy bun and still be the most gorgeous woman to ever walk the earth." My heart fluttered looking at him. I thanked him with my eyes.

"Yeah, yeah. I get that. How about we do a selfie? I'll tag you. We can both get more followers that way, too. Might tick off some of ours that are the opposite sex, though. They will think we are dating." He pulled out his phone, becoming momentarily so immersed by it that it was as if he was the only one alive on earth. Seeing Graham interact with his smart phone was like looking in a house from the outside. My house. My old house, anyway. I did not want to be this person anymore. I wanted to have my head looking up at the world around it.

Graham scrolled for a few minutes, mindlessly, and when Ridge crossed his arms, he suddenly remembered where he was. "Selfie time," he said under his breath, as he opened the camera app.

"Actually, I'm good," I said nonchalantly. Graham was so surprised by this, he pulled his head back in disbelief.

"You don't want to collaborate with me?"

"Can't say that I do. And I'm sorry you came all this way, but I did tell you I was leaving, so that's on you." With that, I turned and walked inside the ranger station, closing the door behind me. And then I waited. My heart was racing from the minor altercation—I'd never been one for confrontation. Heck, I couldn't even confront myself.

Inside the station, I stood up against the wall and watched. In this shaded area, he could see me, but he didn't even try to look inside. For that, I was thankful. I watched the expression on his face turn from shock to anger, and he took the handlebars of his bike and started its small engine.

"You can't have that engine running in the forest," Ridge spoke, sternly but fair. Graham rolled his eyes with the likeness of a child and turned it off as he walked the bike out to the road, disappearing from view.

I ran to open the door as Ridge was walking inside. "I'm so sorry about that, Ridge. I didn't know he was coming."

"That's okay. He seems like a real jerk, if you ask me." I agreed with that sentiment, nodding in reply. But truthfully, I was as much of a jerk as Graham was. Or, at least I had been.

As the wrecker pulled out the remains of my car in the background, I knew the shuttle would be here any time. I didn't want to be rushed when it did arrive, so I started gathering up my thoughts, since I had no possessions to gather.

"Ridge?" I asked as turned to me expectantly. "I just want to say thank you for this experience. It's changed my life in ways that I can't put down in words." He smiled and nodded.

"It changed me, too." I scoffed at the thought of how I could have possibly changed him, but I appreciated the sentiment. As we lingered in our words, the shuttle arrived. I slowly walked to the door, my hand barely reaching the handle when he said my name.

"Ember." I turned back, and he was right behind me, almost as if he was going to kiss me. He didn't, but the moment had more intimacy than I was prepared for. "Be safe." A lump formed in my throat. I thought I was out of tears and yet, they kept coming. I nodded in reply, wanting so badly to reach out and touch his face. Touch his shoulder. Touch his hand. I refrained, and it killed me to do so. But then, I realized I learned something else on this trip that I never knew before: respect.

"Bye, Ridge." I walked outside, leaving the porch, turning back when I reached the van. "If you're ever in Denver, look me up," I said, casually. I couldn't decide if it was welcoming, wanted, or even appropriate to say, but the words escaped my lips. The shuttle driver shut the door behind me as I climbed into the backseat. All I had in my possession was the clothes on my back, a small bag containing the hiking outfit from the ill-fated collab, and a dead cell phone.

The driver climbed back into the driver's seat and moved the rearview mirror so he could see me. He was a dad type, and I felt safe as he put the van in reverse and started driving.

"I estimate we will be at the airport in Cody, Wyoming in under two hours. If you need water, you'll find it in the center console. You can also adjust the air conditioning from the dials in front of you." I thanked the driver for the information. "Call me Dan. Oh, and I almost forgot. This van is equipped with Wi-Fi, and I have charging cords for phones in the console, too." My interest peaked. Wi-Fi? Charging cords? Dared I give it a shot?

My heart started to race, like a kid in a candy store who was just given a taste of salt water taffy when the sugary goodness hit the bloodstream. Little did Dan know, I was a phone addict. I opened the console and sure enough, there was an assortment of charging cables, including the exact one my phone required. It was plugged into a USB port inside, full of juice and ready to boot something up.

My muscle memory reached for my phone instinctively. After it was in my hands, I paused. Was this what I should have been doing? My parents knew that I was inbound. In fact, they were going to pick me up from the airport tonight. I had no real need to connect to this unless it was to check my socials, which I wanted to tread carefully on, since I was addicted to this phone. *No, I shouldn't boot it up*, I thought to myself. My hands were shaking. I wanted to look at the phone. The colors inside. The sounds and videos and attention that was waiting for me on the other end of the internet. I knew I should just let this phone go.

The phone was plugged in a second later. After a minute, signs of life were appearing on the screen. Once I knew the phone wasn't dead, I set it down. With my head in my hands, I prayed for help. To gain control over the object. For healing of my addiction. It wasn't instantaneous. It wasn't easy, either. But

I was able to unplug the cord, sending the screen back to dark. I removed one of my diamond stud earrings and used it to open the SIM card slot on the side of the phone, taking it out and tossing it in the paper bag. Putting my earring back on, I waited for the perfect moment, praying I'd know when it was.

An hour later, we were entering a small community, and Dan asked if I'd like to stop at a rest area. I eagerly said yes. When we pulled in, my eyes were scanning property: gas pumps and a small building where children were sitting outside eating giant soft swirl ice cream cones. I walked into the convenience store awkwardly, Dan waiting at the van for my return. At the back, there was a sign for a restroom, and I made a beeline for it. There was an employee walking out from it with a large, black garbage bag in hand, emptying all of the garbage cans in the building. Another customer asked him a question, and for a moment, he set the bag down. No one was around. I was about to make an irreversible decision, as heaven knew I wouldn't be able to afford a replacement anytime in the near future if I was going to be getting another vehicle. Getting my life back on track was more like it. In a split-second decision, I tossed my phone inside the bag and disappeared into the restroom. A jolt of electricity laced with regret swarmed through my veins. *God, help me now.*

My chin trembled, but the tears wouldn't come—I was fresh out, and my whole being was telling me I did the right thing. But it didn't make it any easier. As I stood at the sink in the bathroom, a woman wearing a name tag came in with a bottle of glass cleaner.

"You look like you've seen better days," she said, spraying the mirror at the sink next to the one I was at. I just let out a sigh in reply.

"You got that right." Splashing water on my face, I reached for the paper towels, cringing at the thinness of them.

"There are few things that an ice cream cone can't fix, sweetie." She winked at me and kept wiping the spotless glass.

"I agree. But I don't have my wallet or any money on me. All of my things were inside my car that got crushed by a tree in Yellowstone." Her eyes widened as she set down the glass cleaner on the sink.

"That was your car? I heard all about that!"

CHAPTER 28
THE LONG WAY BACK
EMBER

Leaving the store a handful of minutes later with a jumbo, soft serve ice cream cone that the woman insisted on buying me, I realized she was right. It was making everything better.

The drive to the small airport in Cody was scenic and beautiful. Mountain ranges in every direction, mixed with herds of deer, elk, and colorful birds flying through the air. If Ridge were here, he could have told me all about these species of animals. My mind fluttered back to him several times as I couldn't help but think of him when I saw all of this gorgeous scenery.

The very snow on the tops of the sprawling mountains reminded me of him and the stories he told me of growing up in the mountains and their winter blizzards. Ridge was a mountain man through and through. I wonder what he was doing now. Did I have it bad, or what?

Finishing my ice cream cone, I was full of the hope that sugar brought and the feeling of peace that I was realizing Jesus provided. Dan told me we were just a few minutes away from the airport. I checked the time; I still had four hours until my flight, but it would feel good to have some alone time to think. When he finally pulled us into the airport, I let out a laugh.

"This is it, huh?" The building was so small, I couldn't see how it even had one gate inside. No long walks were in my future, at least. I was still tired from the jaunt this morning at Lamar Valley.

"Have a safe flight. Thank you for using our service," Dan said, as he opened the van door. I retrieved my small paper bag by its twine handles and stepped out, thanking him.

Inside, I was instantly greeted by employees at a check-in counter and a TSA station when it dawned on me: How the heck could I fly without an ID? I put my palm to my forehead in frustration. Both my mother and I didn't even think of this scenario and here I was. Instead of being stranded in Yellowstone, I was stranded at the airport. Except this one had visiting hours, I was guessing, and I couldn't sleep here overnight.

"Can I help you, ma'am?" I cringed at the words, turning to meet the eyes of a TSA agent whom I told my situation to.

"That was *your* car?" His jaw dropped.

"Yeah, it was me. Anyway, my wallet, purse, all identification was inside. My mom bought me a plane ticket but neither of us considered that, clearly." I let out a tired laugh.

"Hold on. Just a second, alright?" He put his finger up and walked over to his supervisor. After a few minutes of deliberation, the supervisor walked over to me.

"I heard about the car that got smashed in Yellowstone."

"You, too? How does everyone know about it?" He smiled.

"It's a very small town, and word travels fast. Besides, that sort of thing doesn't happen every day." He took off his glasses and wiped them on his tie. "Since it is extenuating circumstances, we can verify your identity another way. Kind of like they do with credit checks. We just get some information from you and go from there." I was so relieved I could cry.

"You mean this can all be behind me now?" My chin trembled, and it seemed very real that I was no longer out of tears. I choked them back, trying to stay professional.

"Yep. As long as we can do our verification process. It's going to take a while, though. Come with me. I'll take you to Anne. Oh, and fair warning: She may look like the sweetest lady you'll ever meet and trust me, she can make some mean turtle brownies, but here at work, she is all business. If any of this is a ruse, she will sniff it out like a bloodhound finding a piece of cheese under Nanna's recliner."

"How specific," I said, agreeing to no funny business. As he led me into a room, he left and returned moments later with some refreshments. A bottle of water, a hot cup of coffee, and some airplane snacks. I was surprised by the gesture.

"This is so kind of you. Thank you." He waved off my words.

"We are all children of God, and you've been through a lot. Do you need anything else?" His words made me tear up, and I didn't know why.

"This—this is great." He nodded and left. I had a few minutes before Anne would arrive and verify my identity. Before she came in, I wanted to get my act together. I smoothed out my ponytail that I had been wearing for several days. My hair was thick and coarse, so I could usually get away with wearing it like that for five days or so with the help of a little dry shampoo but today, it felt wretched. There was no classing up my appearance in this case.

Anne arrived like a hurricane to the room, catching me off guard. The windowless screening room was situated in front of large windows that overlooked the runway and when the door swung open, the beautiful light flooded the room for just a moment. But once the door shut, her smile was the rest of the sunlight that I needed. Not only did I pass the screening, which was stressful as I had to recall old addresses, numbers, and facts about myself that I hadn't thought of in years, but then we started talking about what happened. Before I knew it, I told her the whole story involving Ridge, my phone addiction, and why I came out here to begin with, finishing with my commitment to Christ. Her bright, blue TSA uniform was brilliant in the sterile light.

"It sounds like that, in the end, you found what you were looking for." She nodded.

"What do you mean? I've certainly lost the brand deal, which is why I came out here. And, Graham is a real jerk. I was delusional to think otherwise. And Ridge, well, I'm not ready for something real."

"You came looking for validation, attention, and love. You are leaving with someone who loves you more than you can even comprehend—Jesus Christ." The weight of the words sat between us.

"Wow," I said, wiping a tear from my eye. I am overwhelmed with emotion. "You're so right."

"Mhmmm. You know, I have a grandson that's just like you. He's one of those *influencer* guys online. Poor thing can't do anything without setting up a ring light and camera first now. Last Easter, I invited everyone over to dye eggs with me." She paused, leaning in. "I know it's not a Christian tradition, but the little grandkids just love to stain everything in my house with those awful dye tablets!" I let out a laugh. "Anyway, he came over and was wearing a goofy suit with shorts instead of pants with colorful eggs printed all over them and of course, he had to be front and center doing it. The kids could barely get a turn. Afterwards, I asked him to hide some of the plastic eggs out back, and he had to turn that into some sort of reality television segment. '*Watch me hide eggs for my nanna*' I think he called it. He sent it to me, but I couldn't bear to watch it. That whole day, I thought he looked like a real idiot because of how he was dressed. He said it was all for his followers online. I'm not so sure. I think he's lost a few brain cells along the way."

"I wasn't expecting it to go in that direction." I let out a laugh. Knowing exactly the type of person she was talking about made it even funnier. To the outside world, these people obsessed with their online image, myself included, and did look ridiculous at times.

"If I were you…" Anne started in as she gathered up her papers and rose from her chair. "I would go back." My heart stopped beating for a moment.

"To Yellowstone?" I whispered, thinking of Ridge. She shook her head.

"To Denver. Give God some time to work on you. Stay the course. See what happens." I nodded.

"I feel the same way."

"And if you and Ridge are meant to have something more, well, you'd be surprised at what God can do." Surprised by Anne's words, I tilted my head back.

"I don't know. I'm assuming I will never see him again," I said with a sigh.

"You don't know that."

"True, I don't. But I can't see how that would even happen?" I asked.

"Don't put a limit on God."

"But that would mean Ridge has to wait even longer to find someone, and..." I trailed off.

"It sounds like this man has more patience than there are stars in the sky." She shrugged. "Have a safe journey home, Ember. It was lovely getting to know you." She gave me instructions on what to do next, then left the room, leaving the door wide open for me to do the same. I retrieved my small paper bag and headed to the front, retrieved a boarding pass, and made my way through security.

On the flight home, I was sitting alone. The airport had been small, and the plane was even smaller. There were just two seats to each row on the right, and one seat on the left. It was nice to have some down time to really think.

My heart craved to read through the pages of a Bible. I wondered if I still had one after all of these years. And I wondered what God might be wanting to say to me through it. I couldn't wait to dive in. In just the hours since I recommitted my life to Christ, which was starting to feel like the first time, since I've never felt this way before, I had felt led to more personal changes than I ever had. What could God do through me in a week? A month? A year?

My thoughts went to Traci, my longest friend who'd been undeniably loyal to me when I didn't deserve it. I wanted to do something for her. When I got back, I intended to show her that I was going to change. That she deserved a good friend who listened to her and was selfless like she has been for me all of these years.

Seeing Denver out of the small window reminded me of the adventure I'd been on this week. Anne was right—I came here looking for the validation of others, and I was leaving with a heart renewed in Christ. I decided then that I was grateful I came on this trip. I couldn't regret something that changed me so much or anything that led me to meeting a wonderful man like Ridge. He was sincerely the kindest, toughest, and godliest man I had ever met, and I hoped one day, when God decided that I was ready, I could meet a man like him.

*****

My mom was waiting for me at the pickup zone, right outside the doors of the airport.

"I'm so glad you made it home safe," she said, as she pulled me in for a deep hug. I hugged her harder than I ever had hugged anyone.

"Thank you, mom. For everything you've done to help me. I didn't deserve any of it." She gave me a twisted look as we pulled away.

"You're my daughter. Of course I am going to help you. Even when you are a brat." She smiled, and we made our way back on the freeway.

That night, back in my apartment, after a long, hot shower, I put my freshly washed hair up in a towel. My plush bathrobe felt luxurious on my moisturized skin. My sore feet, blistered from breaking in new hiking shoes all week, screamed in joy as I slipped them into a pair of fluffy socks. And then, I immediately started looking through all of my things until I found it: a pink women's Bible, given to me when I was a teenager. It had barely ever even been opened. For that, I felt remorseful. I opened it up; not putting it down until I read an entire Gospel of Jesus in the New Testament. The words were devoured by my mind and heart. Everything we needed—all of the wisdom of the world—could be found in these pages. And the fact that Jesus died for my sins so that I, too, could be washed clean by the Spirit, brought me to tears a final time tonight.

    Before I went to bed, I prayed for guidance. Direction. Things were such a mess, but through it, I felt hope for the first time in my life.

CHAPTER 29
GOD DOESN'T NUDGE WITHOUT PURPOSE
RIDGE

Ember had been gone for two days. The tree that her car was smashed under was still lying flat; the park crews were coming later this afternoon to clear it. Until then, the campsite was closed. I'd taken it upon myself to clean up the loose debris, which I was pretty sure was in my job description anyway. The loose granola had all but blown away. Pieces of flimsy metal from that pathetic excuse of a tent were everywhere, and bright purple pieces of the vinyl fabric were scattered about. I gathered everything up, throwing them into a black waste bag and thinking of her every second of the day as usual.

It was apparent that Ember and I came from two very different lives. She was a city girl, attached to technology and required cell phone service and a strong data stream at all times. Me, the only streaming I wanted was if I was walking knee deep through one with a fishing pole. Ember was emotional. I was stoic. She was a handful at times—rash, spontaneous. That was how she came out here as unprepared as she did, after all. I planned things for weeks. Months. Years. There was nothing uncalculated about my movements. I was the epitome of tactical, by nature. Still, I couldn't shake the feeling that God didn't want me to give up on this woman. I was drawn to her like I was to nature. And with all of the beauty I was surrounded by, out here in God's country, she was the most beautiful sight I'd ever laid my eyes upon.

Before Ember left, she told me that she'd dedicated her life to Christ. I admitted, that made me feel hopeful. While I didn't think she was an unbeliever before, she hadn't really been serious about it or anything in her life. That was clear to me. I didn't judge her for that, because we were all living for the first time. No one knows what they are doing, but God does. And only He can lead us on the right path.

Still, in that hope, I pushed it out of my heart. I didn't, nor had I ever had any control of the situation. If she was going to be the woman for me, I needed it to happen naturally. I couldn't let myself get in the way of God's plan. And with that, I prayed, reminding God that I was all for His plans and not my own, even if I had to wait another decade to find the woman for me, hoping it would be much sooner than that, of course.

CHAPTER 30
THE QUIET THAT CHANGES YOU
EMBER

As I walked up the street, Traci was waiting for me outside of Le Blanc, a cute Parisian bakery that served delectable chocolate croissants. It had been a week since I'd returned from my Yellowstone adventure and without a phone, the only way I'd been able to call her was from the landline at my parent's house.

"I hope I haven't kept you waiting long," I said, giving her a hug. She looked at me with wide eyes.

"Nope, I just got here about ten seconds ago. You look—*beautiful,*" she said, eyeing my very brightly colored floral silk blouse, paired with white pants and sandals. None of which was tight. As it turned out, looser clothes were super comfortable, stylish, and made me feel more mature. A feeling that I was faking until I made it.

"Thank you. I have a job interview at two," I said, nonchalantly. Traci nearly fell over.

"What? Where? What about the social media stuff? And where are your signature eyelashes, Ember?"

"Yep. It's a full-time marketing job for the State Parks Service. And we have a lot to catch up on," I said with a wink. "My lash extensions fell off while I was in Yellowstone, and I decided it was time for something more natural." I still couldn't say the name without my heart sinking and thoughts of Ridge being there without me. "Oh, by the way. Let me give you my new number," I said, pulling out a small flip phone from my white bucket bag that matched my pants.

"Woah. Retro!" she said, her eyes about to bug out of her head. "That trip really did you good, huh?"

"You have no idea," I said with a laugh. And I told her everything over our two, creamy lattes and heavenly pastries.

"Well, I can't believe it, Ember. You are a Phoenix rising from the ashes. You hit rock bottom but look at you now. On track with life, with God—I couldn't be prouder of you, girl." She put her hand on mine, her sparkling engagement ring dazzling in the daylight.

"Enough about me, Traci. Tell me how the wedding planning is going? Do you need any help with anything?" She paused and nodded.

"Honestly, I need help with everything." She leaned back in her chair. "It was just supposed to be a humble affair. It's at our church. But his family is huge. Like, hundreds of people. So now, we need a reception hall to accommodate, and his parents have offered to pay for the whole thing, which I'm so grateful for. In doing so, they also hired a wedding planner whom I have to meet with at four today, by myself because Chase is working, but he's so encouraging that I just do whatever I want with the day. Even though we have a good budget, I want it to be humble. I'm not looking for it to be the event of the century."

"Want me to go with you?" I asked. Traci looked surprised.

"What? I mean, yes. Yes, I do. I would love that. Thank you, Ember." Her surprise reminded me just what a bad friend I had been to her all of these years. While words fell short, it was time I showed her from now on that I could be there for her.

That evening, a shipment arrived at my apartment. It was the exact camera that I had destroyed at the ranger station. I packaged it into a small box that I had prepared and addressed it to Ridge, sending it to the very ranger station that he reported to every day. I had so many things to say, but every time I tried to write them down in a letter, I fell short. Instead, I just sent the camera, thinking it would be enough words.

I also sent the outdoor brand I was to do a collaboration with a check for the clothing they sent me. I couldn't fulfill the agreement, and I wanted to make it right. Explaining in a letter to them was easier than writing even one word to Ridge, but I said something short.

"Your clothing sent me on an adventure that changed my life."

Four Months Later

Working for the State Parks had been a dream. Not only had working in an office enhanced my people skills, but I'd felt myself living a much more diverse life of socializing in person instead of behind a screen. The office had fun little group hikes every week that we could sign up for. I'd gone more than I ever thought I would. And today, the first Monday of the month, one of my cute co-workers, Nick, asked me out.

"Hey, Ember," he said, quickening his pace to catch up to me in the employee lounge, almost breathless.

"Hey, Nick. Did you have a good weekend?" I asked. He nodded, quickly.

"Yes, I did. Thanks. I tried to find you on social media this week, but I couldn't."

"I'm not on any social media anymore. It was taking up too much of my life." The understatement of the year. Nick raised his eyebrows in surprise.

"Wow, okay. Good for you. Say, I was wondering…" He looked around, lowering his tone. "Would you want to go to dinner with me?" I shook my head like it was a reflex.

"I'm not ready to date," I said. He frowned but took it graciously.

"Bad breakup?"

"No. I'm waiting for God's timing, and this isn't it yet." He didn't say anything, but we both lingered. I was ready to answer any questions he may have thrown upon me, but none came. Eventually, he paced back to his desk. When he was gone, I reflected on my statement. I knew I wasn't ready yet, because I didn't feel the call on my heart. And deep down, no one had or would compare to Ridge.

"Good for you, girl." Sabrina, a curly-haired woman, was suddenly standing behind me at the lounge coffee station, fiddling with the handle on the espresso machine.

"Oops. I didn't realize anyone was here," I said, hoping I didn't embarrass Nick by turning him down. Sabrina shook her head, knowing what I meant.

"He will be fine." She came closer, aware that the walls here were paper thin. "He has been in love with Jessica for two years and now she has a boyfriend. Not that you aren't every man's type, because girl, you are gorgeous. But I think this was a ploy to make her jealous." The gossip was like fire to my ears and more information than I needed to know. I nodded and went back to my desk and said a prayer for the day.

Peering over my desk, I looked out at the large, picture window that we all were staggered around. There were no cubicles here, which I was pleased with considering how much I wanted to see daylight. The view was lovely. Though there were many skyscrapers and buildings, it also had gorgeous, fluffy trees and the giant sky. In the winter months, I'd be able to watch the sunrise from my desk. And, in the deep winter, I'd see the sunset, too. It wasn't something I was entirely looking forward to, but I was also maximizing my weekends now, spending time on outdoor hobbies and church.

After spending a few weeks at different congregations, including Traci's church, I found my home at one that was just a block from my apartment, which was awesome and convenient. I was now involved in the Wednesday night women's Bible study as well. It had been a great blessing for my life and my walk with God.

Since my adventure in Yellowstone, I'd gained so much in my day-to-day life. I'd invested in a set of real hiking attire, looking for something that had all of the features I needed and hiking boots that were good for my foot shape. I even got a set of hiking poles, a sturdy tent, and a can of bear spray, all of which I had yet to use. I planned on taking a real camping expedition next summer with friends.

After the last several months of commuting by public transportation, I saved up enough for a sizable down payment on a used car and was able to secure it without a co-signer. And lastly, I was paying my parents the full rent that they were due, rather than asking them to subsidize me because I was their daughter. It felt so good to be responsible and a good steward of money.

Since downgrading my tech to a flip phone, which had zero texting capabilities, I felt like I'd been set free. Everyone could get a hold of me if they needed to, but they had to call me to do so and the same went for me. Not only was I connecting with friends and family on a deeper level, considering we had to speak, but it saved so much time. What used to take hours to hammer down plans, we could now establish in just a handful of minutes on a call. And I was also gaining more from the conversations; how could I decipher from someone's text that they'd had an awful, miserable day if they didn't tell me? Or, if someone sounded unusually tired in the early afternoon or high strung in the evening? Calls only had helped me become a more conscientious person.

During the day, my new life had been very full. I usually could get away without thinking of Ridge every hour. Sometimes, a few hours went by. My heart longed for a man whom I would never be with. We were too different.

The first few days when I returned from my Yellowstone adventure, he was all I could think about when I wasn't reading my Bible. So, I read it as much as I could, which helped me with my walk with God even more. But I couldn't shake him. There were so many times I wanted to pick up my phone and dial the phone number of the ranger station. The number I only had because my mother had written it down from her caller ID in case she needed to reach me when I was there. The number that she casually gave me a few weeks after I returned when she started to really realize how much I had truly changed.

At the end of the season, Ridge would be returning to Montana, like he told me. This was only a seasonal gig for him. Something he had wanted to try out for some time because he just loved Yellowstone. His love for the park had brought him there. I just wished I had asked him more questions. Where was his family ranch in Montana? What was it called? Not that any of it mattered for me. Ridge and I were opposites in every sense. But I still wanted to daydream about him. He wasn't just the most handsome, masculine, strong man I'd ever met in my life (but that certainly stood out). He was also the kindest, godliest, boldest man. He shared his faith like it was water, pouring over everyone around him. He shared his possessions with me like he didn't care if he'd ever see them again. And he shared his heart. I just wasn't mature enough to receive it.

One chilly day in autumn, I pulled the phone number out of my bedside drawer. My hands were shaking at the thought.

What would I even say to him? *Hey, Ridge. What's up?* Nothing came to mind. I could have told him the truth about me. That I'd changed. I'd given up things, and I'd gained Christ. But would it have even mattered? Maybe he had already moved on. He could have been in a relationship with an outdoorsy ranger woman now for all I knew. I put the number away.

In late October, I pulled it out again. He would be leaving anytime now; I was certain of it. Our seasonal state park rangers only worked until November 1st, so time was of the essence. I decided to go into the call not having anything planned to say. I would just see how he was doing.

As it rang, my heart dropped with every sound. No one answered. I looked at my watch—a handy tool for someone who wasn't looking at a cell phone all day. It was almost lunch time. Perhaps they were all just out on a backcountry patrol? The bears were getting really active right now. Maybe he was fencing off an area. I couldn't wait to see which it was, because I'd learned so much these past months working for the State Park, I felt like I could have really gone toe-to-toe with him. Well, maybe not that much knowledge, but at least I knew you must have bear spray now. A far cry from who I was before.

The ranger station didn't have a Caller ID. Technically, this meant I could call until he picked up. I called again an hour later, but this time, someone answered on the first ring.

"Fishing Bridge Ranger Station," the male voice barked on the other end of the line. *Travis.*

"Oh, hi, Travis. This is Ember. I, um, had the tree fall on my car this spring." If that doesn't narrow it down, I don't know what else to say. His voice softened.

"How could I forget? How are you doing, Ember?" I was surprised to hear him speak so kindly.

"I'm doing great. Really, really great. Thanks for asking." I paused, waiting for him to offer to hand the phone to Ridge who *must have been* sitting right there, right? Wrong. "So, I was hoping to catch Ridge. Is he there by chance?" My voice was high, squeaky, and nervous. I hated it.

"Ridge left about a week ago." His words were final and obsolete. My heart sank.

"Oh, okay. Well, darn. I waited too long to call, I guess." My laughter was weak and doing a very poor job of hiding my disappointment.

"Yeah. Well, take care, Ember. And if you come back to Yellowstone, don't try camping again." His snarky words made me chuckle.

"Too bad, Travis. I already bought a tent. It's a name brand one this time, though. With great reviews. And, I even have a bottle of bear spray."

"Be safe. Bye," he said, hanging up the call. *I waited too long to call.* The words I spoke rang in my head over and over. Except, it was only recently that I had realized I wanted to call. That I was perhaps feeling ready to call. No, that wasn't it. I still didn't know if I felt completely ready for what he had to offer, which wasn't fair to him. I just knew that I was drawn to him across the mountains and states that separated us. I was pulled in his direction. I prayed, giving my feelings up to God. This wasn't an easy thing to feel, my confusion of emotions, but I remembered it was His way, not mine, and that took all of the pressure off, at the very least.

CHAPTER 31
TURNS OUT, I LIKE NATURE
EMBER

The holidays came and went. I participated in a Christmas nativity scene at church. I played the angel of the Lord. All was well until I tripped on the lighting cord and caused the whole room to gasp. When I hopped back up with a bloody nose, I gave my best pageant wave, and everyone clapped. Other than that, and a sore nose for a few weeks, the holidays were quiet. Too quiet. I was starting to feel a longing to find someone. If I hadn't known better, I had even thought I saw Ridge once in the city. But I quickly brushed it off. Just the thought of me seeing him in Denver made me slap my forehead. Did I now know this man at all? He would have rather chewed through leather than be in a place like this. He lived in the mountains and the great outdoors. Still, the thoughts of wanting someone persisted. I knew that winter made everyone couple up, but this feeling was different. It felt like God was telling me that I was ready for a relationship. But the only way I would date was if it led to marriage, because I didn't want anything casual. I didn't want to date just to date.

The cold winter months were painfully slow. Come March, it felt like it was snowing every day. I was forgetting to feel what the sun felt like on my face. I started using the tanning bed at my gym once a week just to get some light rays, which helped immensely. And as the days went on, the desire to find a partner grew inside of me, nagging my heart and mind.

"Okay, Lord. If I'm ready, send me a man," I prayed aloud one morning, as I rose from bed. Without God, I'd only made the wrong choices. Now, it was time to give my dating up to Him and wait.

That morning at work, a flyer for a group snowshoe trip was sitting on top of my keyboard. "Doesn't this look fun?" I said, nudging Carina, who sat next to me. She was the new marketing intern for the department, and we'd really hit it off. She'd even been going to Bible study with me on Wednesday nights.

"It really does. I just don't know if I have anything warm enough. It's supposed to be like ten degrees this weekend." One thing I had learned from my trip was that you have to check the weather and know where you are going. "And look at the location! It's way colder up there in the mountains." All it took was one word to fill my mind with the magical imagery of Ridge, forging through a snowy mountain range on snowshoes.

"I've actually never been to Rocky Mountain National Park," I whispered to her. "Don't tell anyone!" I said with a laugh.

"Me either!" she exclaimed. "That's it. We're going. Together, we can pretend like we know just where we are and that we've been there a million times." She giggled. Truthfully, I didn't care that I was the least outdoorsy person in the office. Everyone had been very gracious and patient with me while I learned the ropes of hiking. I was sure it would be no one's surprise that this would be my first time snowshoeing.

When Carina jumped to sign us up for the snowshoe trip this Saturday, I looked out the window ahead with an anticipation for adventure that felt both foreign and familiar.

After work, Carina drove us to her "favorite outdoor store"-—the same one I bought the tent from last spring—to look for something to wear.

"I have to preface this shopping trip with a word of warning," I said, laughing at the chances that she brought us here. "Remember that Yellowstone trip I told you about, where the tent was very poor quality? It was from here." I shook my head with laughter, but a lump formed in my throat. Suddenly, I felt homesick from that experience.

"This store? I'm surprised. Everything I've gotten here has been really nice." She looked at the store from her car where we were parked outside on the curb. Finding a spot downtown was pretty lucky, especially right in front of where you wanted to go. Maybe it was a sign—or, maybe it was a *bad* sign because no one wanted to shop here.

"Have you ever used any of it in the wild?" She nodded at my question.

"Yeah, definitely. I mean, everything has been gently used, at least." We both giggled and decided to go in anyway. At least to get a starting point. We weren't camping, and it was just a day trip. If our ski clothes ripped to shreds from that, well, at least we would be together.

When we walked in, the feelings I had for missing Yellowstone—and the ranger inside—grew tenfold. Everything reminded me of him. Which was silly because I made the marketing materials all day long for outdoorsy things and places. I'd been to other stores and bought my share of hiking gear. I'd been in the mountains around here and been on several treks, that for all intents and purposes, should have made me think of Ridge more. But today, for some reason, paired with the intense pull I was experiencing that it was time to find a partner, I couldn't think of anything—or anyone—else.

We both settled on one-piece snowsuits. Hers in blue and mine in white. "Are you sure you want white, Ember? What if it's a white out blizzard, and we can't find you?" Her question did make me hesitate. I went back to the rack and again looked at the other colors.

"I don't think I like any of these other ones to be honest." There was a military tan color, a mechanical gray and black. They all felt too utilitarian. Carina had blue eyes, and the blue was just stunning on her, plus, it was the last one. I sighed.

"We just got that same suit in pink," a woman from behind the cash register said. "Let me go get it."

"Pink?" Carina's eyes lit up. "We will look like Easter eggs!" Her excitement was contagious.

The pink was bright. More of a bubblegum color than I had anticipated, but it was better than the rest, and it made my skin look like it had more color to it. The white did wash me out. It wasn't outrageously flattering, but that was no longer the point I was trying to make every single moment of my life, like before. Sure, I wasn't trying to wear potato sacks, but I had leaned into dressing modestly and found I felt even more beautiful than ever. Turned out, nice clothes that fit in the right areas didn't have to be skintight to let you look shapely. You didn't have to show off every inch or curve of your body to be beautiful.

We left with shopping bags full of essentials—the ski suits, hats, mittens, and even some warm socks. We were going to wear our hiking boots inside of the snowshoes since they were already waterproof and plenty insulated. The outfits were set, and she drove me back to my car at the office, just a few minutes away.

"This is going to be so fun," she said, as I got out of the car.

"I agree. See you tomorrow, Carina!"

CHAPTER 32
HOME ISN'T A LOCATION PIN
RIDGE

The days were getting shorter and my daily backcountry patrols were showing much more activity for wildlife as the weather started to cool down even more. Mule deer were going to start to migrate back to their autumn and winter ranges in a few weeks. Bears would be getting as much food as possible before their den season, and the bison, well, they continued to do whatever it was that they wanted.

A chill was in the air today. My mind couldn't drop the idea of returning to the station to grab my coat, as I knew that this chill was going to turn into a very cold afternoon as the clouds rolled in. As soon as I was done checking a forested area around a popular lake for tourists and ensuring that everyone was recreating without the threat of animals or attracting them, I beelined it for the station. When I walked in, the wall phone was ringing. I admitted, ever since Ember left, I hoped it would be her on the other end of the line every time it rang.

I hadn't heard from her since she left. The only way I even knew she made it home was because about two weeks later, I received a package from her. No note, no return address. Just a camera. I wanted to send it back. To tell her to return it, because I already replaced it. But with no return address, I held onto it, keeping it as a reminder that she existed in the first place.

Racing to answer the phone, I hoped for her voice on the line. But it was my boss, Bob.

"Hi, Ridge. Do you have a second?" His voice sounded serious. And even after all of these months, the disappointment in my voice was palpable.

"Yes, of course. What's going on?"

"This is something a little out-of-the-blue, and I'm sorry to spring it on you like this, but here at the National Park Service, sometimes we shuffle people around like a chess board."

"Okay," I said, unsure of where this was going.

"In our neighboring state, at Rocky Mountain National Park, we've had two backcountry rangers request transfers, one retired and one injured this season. Winter is looking a little slim. I know you are just here with us seasonally, but you seem to enjoy it so much that I was wondering if you'd be interested in such an assignment of spending the winter there."

"In Rocky Mountain National Park?" I asked, dumbfounded at the chances of this phone call.

"Yes. Ninety minutes outside of Denver. But I know what you're thinking: too close to the city. I'm not a city guy either, so if you aren't interested, I can ask Travis." My mind wasn't computing the information fast enough.

"So, I would be just a ways from Denver?" I asked rhetorically, no longer talking to Bob. If this wasn't God pulling strings, I didn't know what was. Bob laughed.

"I take it, you have an interest in Denver." Bob may have been wise, but I didn't take him for a psychic.

"Perhaps," I said with a laugh. "I'll do it. Thank you for the opportunity, Bob."

"That's fantastic, Ridge. This does mean giving up your post in Yellowstone a tad early, though. I want the summer rangers in Colorado to train you on their terrain for a few weeks—not that you'll need it, but I want to set you up for success." The thought of leaving Yellowstone, a place I was secretly hoping that she would return to, had my heart in a twist. But, if anything, now I'd be even closer to her, and I agreed to it.

*****

Whoever thought that city life was better than being a pioneer in the mountains, they should have given me a call. I had a bone to pick with them. In the middle of the dead winter, I thought it might have been interesting to spend a few days in the city. To see what all the fuss was about. I had the time off required, and all of my winter wool socks were getting a little thin. Meteorological spring was just around the corner, but in the Rockies, that meant wet snow and cold temperatures.

I found a hotel downtown that was centrally located to all of the shops, markets, and even a small church. I thought it would do me good to worship with music for a change. While I was out in the field, I worshipped just with my heart, on my own. Don't get me wrong; it was my favorite way of honoring God, but I yearned for that small, intimate experience.

The weekend was uneventful. Other than an outfit stationed outside of my hotel called *Crumbl*, and a farmers market turning a parking lot into a village on a weekend, I did not see the pull of city life whatsoever. The church service was nice, however. Strolling the streets at night, I could never get enough fresh air. It felt too congested from buildings and traffic. And yet, I kept walking. Hoping to catch a glimpse of the woman that I just couldn't shake. The complicated, emotional, beautiful, sweet woman I spent time with in my favorite place. As I walked the streets, I wondered if these were the routes she took. If these were the places that she shopped. On my last morning in the city, I was gazing into a leather store, dreaming of getting a new saddle. The store was closed on Sundays, as it should have been. As I peered into the glass, I caught the reflection of someone who looked just like her. For a moment, our eyes met in the reflection. But when I turned, her back was to me, and she was getting onto a bus. The bus pulled away.

*****

Months went by at my post in Rocky Mountain National Park. I enjoyed the wilderness landscape, but my heart felt unsettled. I felt God nudging me toward something, but He hadn't told me yet what it was. I was in a season of waiting — for what was undetermined.

We had quite a few winter recreators in the area I was in. Now that spring had come, I was seeing more groups of Nordic skiers, snowshoers, and winter hikers going by. It was a lot less lonesome here than the end of the season in Yellowstone was, but I couldn't tell yet if I liked that. Some of the rangers were tasked with doing guided winter trips on Nordic skis and snowshoes. Most days, I felt more like a keeper of the land than I did a ranger. Either the weather had been so treacherous I couldn't get out, or I was just plowing snow around the buildings. I felt a little stir crazy by it all, and suddenly, I wondered if I should take another trip back to the city. This was not a feeling I was comfortable with nor was it one that I was expecting.

Just toying with the idea in my head brought me some relief. If I wasn't here, I'd be back home. We had a small town that I could access with a farm store, groceries, and so on. Though I rarely went to town, I had decided that I was comfortable with the fact that I could. But as I wrestled my mind to find the difference of being in these mountains versus the mountains at home and why I was just so unsettled, I realized it was because my life before meeting Ember was different. I had never met a woman who challenged me in the ways she had done. And finally, I prayed to God and asked what I'd been pushing away all of these months: a chance to talk to her again, if it was His will.

*****

The only reason I knew it was a Saturday was because I marked each day off in my calendar with an "X," so I could keep track. I was off duty today, and I had just two weeks left of my winter post out here. I was ready to finish up. And today, I felt more adrenaline than dread about heading into civilization. Maybe I could find her. I had her name—perhaps I could ask around in a very non-creepy way.

As I walked out of my ranger station, after sending out a message to my co-workers that I would return first thing Monday morning, I saw a band of people heading my way on snowshoes. The trail went right past my station, and I had to take part of the trail on foot to get to my vehicle.

As they got closer, I saw the ranger was Greg. He was one of my favorite co-workers; he always had a smile and a high five to give out. He made everyone's day brighter by being around him. Just seeing him, I knew I wanted to wait a moment so I could say hi and wish him a good trip. Tell him about my plans. I loitered for a minute— he had at least ten people with him. Two women in the back were wearing very brightly colored snowsuits, and it made me smile.

When Greg reached me, half of his group was struggling to keep up. "Hey, man. I'm off for the weekend. Have a great time out there," I said, receiving his high-five with a chuckle.

"We are going to have a blast. This might be the best conditions we've had all season. You're welcome to join us, if you want." Greg's invitation stood still as the rest of the group caught up, and I saw the most beautiful woman wearing a bright pink ski suit. My face froze in shock. Greg turned to look behind him, acknowledging Ember, and turning back to me. "We can wait while you get ready."

Ember hadn't looked up at me yet. She was giggling hysterically with her friend who wore an even brighter blue suit, as they commiserated about their clunky steps in the snowshoes. But the laughter quieted. The world fell silent. Ember, in her thick wool cap over her long blonde hair, looked up at me. And at that moment, my knees weakened and I thanked God. He brought us back together. Ember stomped over to me, taking wide strides in the snowshoes. We stared at one another for a few minutes, both of us without words.

"It's you," she said, and I stood back up, towering over her small frame. In the background, the group shuffled away at Greg's prompt to give us some privacy. She wasn't wearing a stitch of makeup. Her face had filled out a little, and she had a glow of happiness to her.

"I've been praying for another chance to see you. And here you are," I said, my voice shaking. I wrestled with both the disbelief and belief that God was a God of miracles, such as this.

"I tried to call you, but Travis said you already left." Her words were cracking from tears that were pooling in her big, beautiful green eyes.

"I came here. They offered me a winter post, and I took it."

"Here?" she asked, in disbelief.

"It was closer to you." And our bodies hugged. I didn't know who embraced first, but we held on to one another like we were each a life preserver.

We spoke both with words and without for some time, her standing there in her snowshoes and pink suit. Her teeth started to chatter from the cold, and I offered to walk with her while she caught up with the group, so she could warm up.

"I'd love that," she said, linking her arm with mine. As we walked, she told me everything that had changed in her life. The mountains that God had helped her move with overcoming her social media and phone addiction, going to church, and getting a new job. Dressing differently. Even eating more whole foods, like we did when we were in Yellowstone together. It sounded like the season of waiting wasn't just for me.

Just talking to her, I could see the maturity that she had gained in the months we'd been apart. I fell for her before, but now, I was blown away by her. She was a dynamic, thoughtful, and charismatic force to be reckoned with and just seeing her at this stage in her life, I was drawn to her more than ever before.

As we approached the group, she stopped and turned to me. "Ridge," she said, boring into my eyes.

"Ember?" I waited for her to speak, but she hesitated. The more I searched her eyes, the more I felt God speaking to me through them. Ember was to be my wife. I felt that with my whole being now. I prayed she felt the same. And that we could pick things up where we left off.

"I was wondering if you'd like to have my phone number." She reached into her pocket and pulled out a flip phone. I let out a deep laugh.

"My wall phone has a long cord that I can twirl in my fingers while we talk," I said, causing her to laugh with me.

My heart sang the glory of God, in all that He had done in my life.

EPILOGUE
TWO SETS OF TRACKS
EMBER

18 Months Later

The sound of the waves lapping in the close distance woke me. Ridge wasn't in the tent and when I heard the campfire crackling, I knew he was up. I pulled a hoodie over my bedhead, unzipped the very sturdy zipper of our backcountry tent, and met his eyes.

"Good morning, wife," he said, a grin taking over his face.

"And good morning, husband," I said, scanning the fire. "I thought there would be coffee. Don't tell me you tricked me into marrying you by promising a French press every morning." He laughed.

"You know very well we are making campfire coffee on this trip. You picked out the brew, after all." He came and handed me a hot, steaming cup of coffee in a white camping metal mug that said, *Mrs.,* as Ridge drank from one that read *Mr.* They were a gift from Traci and her husband, Chase. "A perfect gift for those who decided to go camping in Yellowstone for their honeymoon," she had told me at our last get together.

"Come see the sunrise, Em," Ridge affectionately called to me. My phone buzzed in the background. Instead, I grabbed the handheld Polaroid camera that I had bought special for this trip.

As I walked out onto the shore, the rough sand below my bare feet, Ridge put his arm around me, and I relished his embrace as I snapped a picture of the beautiful morning. I held up the Polaroid, waiting for it to develop. Ridge turned and gave me a kiss. The Polaroid fell to the ground. "Let's look at that later," he whispered, as he leaned into my lips, kissing me softly and holding me close.

As Ridge and I embraced on the beach, he suddenly pulled away. "Look at that," he pointed to the sand. I picked up the Polaroid.

"The picture?" It was gorgeous but didn't do the sunrise justice. Life was much better experienced firsthand.

"No," he shook his head. "The prints, right next to it." I looked down with a gasp. Large paw prints were traced in the sand.

"Are those... wolf prints?" I asked, feeling like the question might have been silly, as they could have belonged to a coyote or even someone's dog. We weren't the only guests in Yellowstone, but we were in a remote area. In fact, we had yet to see another group near us.

"Yes, they are from a wolf. Look at the size of them." Ridge leaned down, putting his large hand next to it. It was clear it couldn't have been any other species. "And there are two pairs of prints. See? These ones are just a little bigger." We both looked at the prints in wonder, our eyes following the tracks as far as they went before disappearing into the water.

Ridge took my hand and led me down the beach.

ABOUT THE AUTHOR

Cassandra discovered her passion for writing at the age of seven when she purchased a diary at the Scholastic Book Fair. What began with journal entries about her school and home life later evolved into a collection of poems, short stories, and novels. Her hobbies include skiing, traveling around the Rocky

Mountains, and reading. Much of her writing inspiration stems from her love of dogs, her Onondaga heritage, and her Christian faith. Cassandra's favorite genres of books are Christian fiction novels, Thrillers, and anything British.

She is a full-time writer and resides in the mountains of Wyoming with her husband, Chad.

Find her online at cassandrajoelle.com

OTHER BOOKS BY CASSANDRA

Howdy, Handsome: An All-Space, No-Spice Christian Romcom

Houston, We Have A... Meet-Cute.

When a test flight goes sideways, astronaut Jack Carter crash-lands in the last place he expected: the middle of a Wyoming cattle ranch. Dazed, suffering from amnesia, and drop-dead handsome- he can't remember his mission- or even his own name.

Enter Annie McGraw, a cowgirl who doesn't have time for stray cattle... Let alone stray astronauts. But when she takes him in, sparks fly faster than a rocket launch. Out under Wyoming's star-filled skies, Jack launches into a mission he never trained for: a woman who just might be his greatest adventure yet, and a faith that grounds him more than gravity ever could.

Genre: Christian Romantic Comedy

The Chalet Next Door: An All-Ski, No-Spice Christian Romcom

Blizzard Outside. Banter Inside. Sparks Inevitable.

Bubbly book publisher Presley Astor has been told all her life she's "too much." But she's perfectly happy being herself- and taking her pampered Shih Tzu, Priscilla, on a solo ski trip to Sage Mountain, Wyoming. What she's not prepared for is a blizzard knocking out her power and forcing her to seek refuge in the chalet next door...with a brooding cowboy who clearly doesn't know what to do with someone like her. Ford Prescott is a guarded skijoring champion-a rodeo sport where a horse pulls a skier at breakneck speeds-preparing for the biggest race of his life. But he's also fighting cheating competitors and a faith that's quietly slipping through his fingers. As snow piles high and the town shuts down, Presley's joy (and Priscilla's undeniable charm) begins melting Ford's walls. But when old insecurities and misunderstandings hit harder than the storm, they'll have to decide if God's plan for them is bigger than just surviving the blizzard.

How to Fall for a Cowboy: An All-Pumpkin, No-Spice Christian Romcom

She's Glossy Nails. He's Flakey Crust. The Plan? Half-Baked.

In the town of Maple Haven, Wyoming, Autumn isn't just a season- it's a celebration. Ginger Hart is spending the season like she has for the past year: hopelessly crushing on Dallas, the gym bro who communicates in motivational quotes. In her quest for his attention, Ginger's lost more than a few pounds- maybe, a bit of herself. As the town gears up for the annual Pumpkin Stampede, something (or rather someone) rolls into town in a pumpkin-themed dessert truck parked right outside Ginger's salon. Behind the counter? Ex bull-rider Tucker Callahan. He's all cowboy hat and delicious sweets- basically everything Ginger's been trying to resist. When they decide to fake date for his image and for her to get Dallas' attention, he proposes one sugary-sweet condition. As cozy sparks fly, Ginger begins to wonder if God's sweetest plans aren't always the ones we bake up ourselves.

Genre: Christian Romantic Comedy

A Weather Girl's Guide to Love: A Thunderously Sweet Christian Romcom

Partly Cloudy, Mostly Complicated.

Hailey Sinclair had her life all mapped out- until God changed the forecast. Instead of being an on-air meteorologist for a national network, she's reporting the weather in rural Wyoming. Now she's caught between her college sweetheart, Jett Dawson, and Colt Wilder- the infuriatingly gorgeous and cheerful cameraman who seems determined to break through her stormy exterior. Torn between the future she planned, and the one God might be writing, Hailey must learn to trust His direction- and her heart- even when it leads straight into the eye of the storm.

Genre: Christian Romantic Comedy

A New Leash on Life: A Dog-Mom Rom-Com, Book 1

Get ready for a hilarious Christian romantic comedy as we follow the journey of a thirty-something introverted woman, Katie Fitzgerald, who's longing for a husband. But when she accidentally adopts a dog, she discovers that love comes in unexpected ways, and that God's timing is always perfect.

Genre: Christian Romantic Comedy

Fetching Love: A Dog-Mom Rom-Com, Book 2

Three couples, three journeys, and one hilarious adventure on the unpredictable path to love. Katie and Eli are ready to say "I do," but the days leading up to the wedding are full of surprises- especially when Katie's mom's true crime sleuthing lands her in a pickle. Samantha and Mitchell seem perfect together, but hidden struggles test their relationship. Can they find common ground, or will their opposing desires pull them apart? Carolyn and Micah have found faith and each other, but their surprise romance leads to a sudden, life- altering decision. As these couples follow the Lord, they find joy and laughter along the way.

Genre: Christian Romantic Comedy

The Après-Ski Proposal: A Romcom About Love Off- Piste

She came for a fresh start... Not a fake boyfriend. When Claire Riley gets dumped on the eve of her 30th birthday, she's blindsided. A spur-of-the-moment ski trip seems like the perfect escape, until she runs into her ex... With his new girlfriend. Shocked and desperate for a lifeline, Claire accepts a proposal from a charming stranger to pose as her fake- boyfriend. What begins as a simple act of saving face turns into a journey that reveals a fresh start in life and love—the kind that only God could have planned.

Genre: Christian Romantic Comedy

The Curse of Josephine Bagley

Over the course of a century, three individuals are woven together by a decades-old curse:

William, after surviving an Indian raid on his orphanage due to his facial disfigurement, goes on to live among the tribe. But when misfortune befalls them, he is quickly traded away and faced with a pivotal choice that changes his life forever.

Josephine has faced immense loss. Despite her granddaughter's efforts to help her find solace in faith, she finds she can't let go of the past and falls further into her belief that she's eternally bound to darkness.

Saraphina, a fledgling antiques dealer, gets the surprise of her life when a courier delivers notice that she's the last surviving relative of the Bagley Estate. What seemed like a windfall that could help her career now causes her to question her own reality.

In this tale of intertwining mystery, loss, and faith, these souls navigate through nefarious trials to find the gift of grace and forgiveness that extends to us all.

Genre: Christian Gothic

www.ingramcontent.com/pod-product-compliance
Lightning Source LLC
LaVergne TN
LVHW041905070526
838199LV00051BA/2509